Pate and Faircloth

Book 1

Wherefore Art Thou, Jane?

Jean James
and
Mary James

Wherefore Art Thou, Jane?
Copyright © 2013 Woodrock House
Cover art copyright © 2013 by Woodrock House
Book designer Karen Polka
Cover Art by Frank James

All rights reserved. Except for brief excerpts for reviewing, no part of this book may be reproduced or transmitted in any form or by any means, electronic or mechanical, including photocopy, recording, or any information storage or retrieval system, without permission in writing.

Inquiries should be addressed to:
Woodrock House
13097 Hwy. 45 N.
Finger, TN 38334
http://www.woodrockhouse.com
ISBN-978-0-9848605-2-4
Printed in the United States of America

We would like to express
our appreciation to

Frank James
Karen Polka

Other books
by the authors:

Sparrow Alone on the Housetop

God Knew There Would Be a Today

Chapter 1

Never wear dusty boots to meet an Italian Jacket.

"I'm Jane Pate. I called about picking up my check."

She had hoped to step in, grab the check, and run. Who would have thought such extravagant luxury loomed on the other side of that unpretentious, oak door. Self-consciously she glanced down at her work clothes and boots. The secretary had started to search through a pile of papers on her desk when a striking man, mirroring the office that housed him, stepped into the room.

"Anna, did you manage to get the police report on Victor's death? I can't help but wonder if I've failed someone—again. I . . . what is that frightful odor? It smells musty in here."

Jane backed away a couple of steps and held her hands behind her. Before coming into the office, she had transferred one of her snakes to a different bag, and it had left its scent on her hands. She hadn't noticed it till that instant. The scent had always seemed rather agreeable, slightly pungent but definitely not a frightful odor. It resembled the smell of money to her. It meant another collected snake and a few more dollars in a dwindling bank account.

"Mr. Faircloth, this is Jane Pate who is writing that Florida reptile and amphibian book for you. Do you have her expense check? She called yesterday about it."

"Reginald Faircloth—how do you do, Jane?" He seized her unwilling hand and crushed it in a hearty handshake. To her horror, he didn't release it but brought it close to his face and sniffed interestedly. "I believe I've found the culprit. Are you wearing a new perfume, or do you, perhaps, own a pet skunk?"

"Perfume of course—Essence of Snake Musk." She had tried to sound witty, but no one laughed. "I'm sorry if it is offensive. I brought some snakes with me to sell at the zoo. One tried to escape through a hole in its bag, and . . . and I . . ." At that low point, she wished she had never come.

"Oh, indeed, I thought you only required photographs for this project. I didn't realize we were publishing a live book. Or are you creating *scratch and sniff* pages? Do you also write?"

His amused, somewhat-amiable expression belied the impertinent words that rolled forth so easily with slight English accent and no hint of embarrassment. Jane pushed a hand through the short mass of curls that usually framed her head adequately but now hung wet and saggy from the scorching, outside heat. Was this man in jest or had he insulted her?

Before she could reach any conclusions, he turned his attention to a checkbook on Anna's desk. Furtively she studied his attire and grew more ill at ease. She hadn't expected to meet her publisher here at his Panama City location—especially not such a publisher. The immaculate white silk shirt and Italian suit proclaimed that if he were a watch, he would most certainly be a Rolex.

Mentally she scolded herself for no forethought. She shouldn't have come to his publishing house straight from the woods and dressed in her reptile-collecting clothes. She had read in a news article about his grand estate and auspicious publishing house back in London and should have expected something similar here. Furthermore, she should have realized he might actually come here at times—this dreadfully different man from the one she had pictured. Now this platinum-plated smarty mocked her industrious efforts to earn a living.

"You know I couldn't survive on just my expense money." At once, she regretted her poor choice of words and struggled to fill the sudden silence. "I collect reptiles for antivenom laboratories and reptile parks. That way I don't have to worry about a job while I finish the book. And . . . and sometimes I get better pictures if I bring the reptiles home and use different lighting."

"Are you expressing dissatisfaction with the size of your expense check? You know I rarely pay expenses of writers on assignment."

When he handed her the check, she wasn't sure how to take this man and his bluntness. If that was hidden humor in his eyes, it was humor at her expense. She tried to control her rising temper. No need to make him angry—there might not be another publisher interested in her book. At a loss for what to say, she stared down at the floor. His shoes looked Italian too. They made quite a contrast to her . . . She quickly looked up and discovered that his gaze had followed hers and now stared aghast at her boots—her shabby, dusty old engineer boots that had actually worn through in spots.

"I say now, maybe the check *isn't* enough."

"They're my work boots. They just look bad. I didn't get any dirt on the carpet."

"How is it progressing?" He stepped closer and looked at her questioningly.

Thoroughly ill at ease now, it took her a minute to realize he had changed the subject and had only asked about the book.

"Wonderful!" She smiled and hoped her enthusiasm would make up for her belated reply. "I have some excellent pictures—unusual ones. It won't be a typical nature guide or . . . or just another textbook." When no answering comment came, she grew uneasy again and started to leave. "Thank you. It was nice meeting you. I have to take those reptiles to some place cooler. These hundred degree temperatures we've been having can kill them if I'm not careful."

"Jane."

She turned back uneasily.

"Jane—be careful. I would feel deuced uncomfortable if you got snake bit in some inaccessible spot and wasted all that expense money."

"If a spot were inaccessible, I couldn't be in it," she jabbed back, "and I doubt my demise would put you in the poorhouse."

She stood straight as she turned again to leave. The last thing she saw when she closed the door was a broad smile on the face of that impossible man. She groaned to herself. What had she done? She made up her mind to transact all future business with him by mail. Anyway, there would be no more checks until the book was completed. This money would have to last. Sliding onto the hot seat of her truck, she glanced down at the check. It was made out for the correct amount all right, but it wouldn't do her much good until he signed it.

After beating her head against the steering wheel, she sighed helplessly, glad that no one could see her from the office window. She had purposely parked where no one would notice her tired looking vehicle. The compact truck had not served faithfully, or even adequately, but it was the best she could afford. She didn't want anyone to think less of her because of a few rust spots or the wispy smoke it now emitted regularly. At least her publisher hadn't seen that, she told herself as she headed back to the office with her useless check.

An empty secretary's desk and a heavy odor of floral spray greeted her when she timidly reentered the office. She waited for Anna's return and avoided making any noise that could invite a second encounter with the publisher. When sounds of movement in a nearby room drew her attention, she walked over and glanced in the open door expecting to find Anna putting away a can of air freshener. She found no one in that room either, at least no one at the desk. Mr. Faircloth occupied the plush carpet beside his desk where he proceeded with a brisk-paced set of pushups, though his face had now turned in her direction. Her common sense told her that many people seized moments of exercise when time and opportunity allowed, but as his eyes continued to study her, she felt compelled to fill the silence—again.

"Did you lose something, sir?"

Knowing she couldn't outdo the stupidity of those words, she let the awkward silence reign while he leisurely stood, replaced his cuff links and intimidating jacket, and brushed some invisible lint from his pants.

"I was indulging in a bit of exercise, Jane. Since I'm a publisher and not a writer, I have to find ways to stay fit. I don't have time to tramp through the woods and daisy pick for my health and recreation."

"If you *reptile picked* with me, even once, you'd see how

unrecreational it is."

The words had hardly left her mouth before she wished she could recall them. They had leaped out all by themselves to fill the uncomfortable silence with this man.

"Excellent idea. I could use a change of scenery."

Anna came to his open door and looked surprised to see Jane there.

"Excuse me. I didn't realize you were in conference."

"That's all right, Anna. Jane and I are planning a field trip."

"Mrs. Torne is on the phone and wants to talk with you. She says she has new reason to believe the fire wasn't an accident."

"Thank you, Anna. I never thought it was an accident. Tell her I'll call back."

He stared at his desk for a minute before he shook off whatever vision had temporarily invaded his thoughts. When he looked up at Jane, remnants of distress still lay deep in his eyes.

"I lost one of my writers a short while ago—in a house fire. The incident has . . . troubled me. But we must get on, mustn't we? How about tomorrow?"

She stood there speechless. She hadn't actually invited him, had she? Who would have dreamed he would want to go? No way could she snake collect with her publisher—not this publisher. Nervously, she turned the tiny pearl ring on her left hand and searched for appropriate words.

"It won't offend the trinket profferer if we go off into the woods alone, will it? Do I need to call him for permission?"

"My engagement ring, you mean?" She began to grasp that this man's eyes missed nothing. "His name is Cody Strickland. Of course he won't mind." In defense of the ring, she held out her hand as if displaying a rare diamond, "It was his mother's ring."

"Passed away?"

"N-no."

"Oh, he stole it from her costume jewelry." His eyes danced and invited a brawl.

"I don't think you'd enjoy a reptile hunt." This irrepressible man exasperated her. "It's hot, dirty work."

"Hot and dirty sounds fine to me. And I'm not fortunate

enough to have someone to call for permission."

The silence lingered uncomfortably long as she took in the Oxford plaque smugly flaunting its presence on the wall behind his mahogany desk.

"Maybe . . . just for a morning. I usually rough it—no picnic lunches, no cold drinks."

"I want it served exactly the way you relish it. I seldom take a day off, so I hope you can offer me a full day's entertainment."

"Tomorrow morning I collect up near the Alabama line. I planned to float down Wrights Creek that afternoon for water snakes and turtles."

"I'll try not to get in your way." He spoke humbly, but that distressing twinkle remained in his eyes. "What time should I come to your house?"

"Let's meet somewhere in Bonifay," she rushed to suggest. He mustn't see her house. "That will work better. My home is very difficult to find."

He flipped through an address file on his desk and pulled out Jane's card.

"Here's your place, about fifty or sixty miles from here." His face gleamed with satisfaction.

"Yes. That's me. . . . I'll leave about five-thirty in the morning."

She felt a little bewildered as she left his office for the second time. Not until she had climbed back into her truck did she realize she still held the unsigned check. She crammed it into her purse and drove away.

When she reached home, she panicked. He intended to meet her there—her publisher. He would see her house, her truck, everything. She would have to work incredibly fast to make her place look presentable by morning. There hadn't been much home time lately, and the computer ate up most of that. She hurried into the house, changed into shorts and a halter-top, and rushed back outside.

One frantic look at the uncut grass in the large yard told her where to begin. Recent rains had sent the vegetation to unbelievable heights, knee-high and above, and had turned the flower beds into tangled masses of weeds.

She pulled the lawn mower from under the house and

wondered if the ancient piece of rusted metal could handle the job ahead. She had jerry-rigged everything on it. The muffler had abandoned it the last time she mowed, a piece of coat hanger wire secured the gas tank to the motor, and the pull cord mechanism had suffered a hernia. She now had to wrap the cord around it manually each time she pulled it. The throttle cable had escaped too, but she had tied the carburetor open so the engine stayed on constantly—high speed only. That made it necessary to push the mower into tall grass or knock the spark plug wire off in order to kill the motor. Otherwise, it would run until it used up the gas. At least the mower had never failed to run.

Confidence soon turned to desperation as she coaxed the mower to show some sign of life. After she had exhausted her strength, all the tricks of her limited mechanical ability, and thirty minutes of precious time, she gave up and left it on her front walk. The electric Weedeater would have to cut the grass. At least she had paid her electric bill.

The grass cutting progressed slowly. She wiped her forehead and wished she lived in a nice apartment, not an old frame house with tons of upkeep. But apartments were expensive and wouldn't accept her menagerie of reptiles and amphibians. That concern took priority now that the collecting had become her total support, though she hoped the book might soon contribute a bit to her revenue. She planned to write it and many more—as soon as she made it through tomorrow's terrible ordeal with her publisher.

Wet with sweat, her head a forest of damp ringlets, she paused to survey the work. The small spot of yard she had finished gave the appearance of cut hay. The grass lay in deep mounds across it and would require hours of raking when she finished cutting. She sighed audibly. Hot, tired, and totally peppered with chopped grass, she observed that the string cutter had overheated too. It would have to cool off even if she had no time for such luxury.

She left it beside the mower and turned her attention to her dusty truck. It badly needed a bath. Armed with a bucket of sudsy water and some rags, she took a minute to turn the hose on her baked head, arms, and finally her entire body. It refreshed her, but it didn't remove the grass that clung tenaciously to her skin and clothes.

Now I resemble a wet, scrawny version of the Hulk, she thought amusedly and took a long drink from the hose.

It took only minutes to work her way around the vehicle with a rag. Though it did improve the appearance of the beige paint, now the rust spots stood out blatantly. She tried to ignore them and started work on the interior. Everything had to be perfect for her exalted guest. He would probably ride with her. With that thought in mind, she turned the hose on the interior of the cab, blasting seats, windows—everything. When satisfied with the job, she left it open for the hot sun to dry.

The dirtiest task still awaited her—the truck's mechanical needs. At least the bucket still contained a few inches of soapy water. While she brought the truck's fluids up to the proper level, yellow flies came out of nowhere and lit on her wet skin—lit and bit. She Knew she painted many, greasy, black smears on her skin as she swatted them away from her face and neck but at that point she didn't care. Finally, she replenished the power steering fluid and ended up with black smudges on her right arm up to her shoulder.

Just as she replaced the cap, a long, dark-brown Lincoln Continental pulled into her grass-covered drive. She looked at it from under her hood. No doubt someone needed directions or was turning around. She pulled blackened fingers away from the engine and pushed the dripping curls off her forehead with the back of her hand. Horrified, she heard the engine stop and watched Mr. Faircloth get out.

No. No, she thought, and gazed aghast at the chaos around her.

Chapter 2

*Never invite a Lincoln Continental home
unless you have mowed your yard.*

"You're a little early, Mr. Faircloth."

She managed to say it sweetly and knew she deserved an Oscar for her outstanding portrayal of a calm, rational human being.

"I thought it best to find lodging in Bonifay to avoid the drive in the morning."

He stopped abruptly and took in the entire scene. His eyes opened wider, and she wasn't sure if it was horror she saw there or something else.

"Yes?"

"I drove by so I could be sure I had the correct place."

"If it still seems correct to you, then this is it. I'm working at a bit of neglected clean-up."

"Could I trouble you for a drink of water?"

Jane froze. She glanced in the direction of her house, and her mind registered a quick negative. With her not-so-blackened left hand, she held the hose out to him.

"I'm sorry, Jane, I didn't realize Cootie would be home. I didn't mean to embarrass you. The hose will do nicely. You needn't ask me in."

In spite of his words, he never took the hose from her outstretched hand, but stood there with an expectant look on his face and studied the house.

"*Cody* . . . doesn't stay here. I'd invite you in but . . ."

"But your house needs a 'bit of neglected clean-up'?"

"I haven't been home much lately."

"Can't Cootie help with some of this?" His gesture of despair included the whole impossible scene that she had unwittingly prepared for his viewing.

"It's *Cody*—not Cootie. Cody works in Louisiana. He only gets back to his home in Panama City every other weekend."

She stooped to wash the engine grease from her hands.

"You have some on your face too. Hand me the rag and . . ."

"Would you like to come in?" she interrupted and dropped the rag in the bucket. "I'll fix you a glass of lemonade. Please excuse the house. I haven't had time to clean it recently."

"Thank you. A spot of lemonade would go nice."

She took him into her kitchen. She knew that would be the neatest place in the house since she hadn't cooked anything in ages. While they sat at her kitchen table and sipped icy lemonade, she began to recoup her self-esteem—that is, until he began to scrutinize the room too closely.

"You know, Jane, I have somewhat of an idea about this dirty house thing that bothers you. Faircloth Publishing was founded on rather strong moralistic and humanitarian ideals. We maintain the theory that while we can't hope to make everything around us clean and perfect, we can strive to create a sparkling spot in a sometimes dingy environment. We do our small part to make a . . . a better world. I guess that's the best way to put it. You know, like clean a room even though the rest of the house remains dirty." When he glanced once more around her kitchen, she felt ready to commit murder.

"Actually, that's my philosophy too, but when there's no time to clean a room, I concentrate on being clean myself. That way I can be the bright spot in a dingy world."

He reached for a small mirror that rested on a shelf and held it in front of her. Mirrored back to her was a drooping pile of golden-brown curls, two large brown eyes with shock registered plainly in them, and the most grease-streaked, grass-streaked face she had ever beheld. She batted the mirror away.

"I was referring to *inside* clean."

"I understand, Jane—really." He struggled to control his laughter. "But you are rather a mess. I hope I haven't been the cause of this cleaning eruption."

"No, of course not," she lied. "I finally had an evening at home and was trying to catch up. But it's rained so much, and the mower wouldn't start."

"That's hard luck. Let me look at the blasted thing. Maybe I can coax it into action."

"No . . . n-no . . . really. I'm ready to quit for the day," she lied again, scared stiff he might see her lawn mower. "I intend to write for a while and then catch up on sleep." If it was necessary to tell a falsehood, she might as well say what a publisher should want to hear from one of his writers.

"Well, if you're entirely certain. I'll be back here at five-thirty in the morning."

She watched him wade back to his car through the cut grass. He stopped at her lawn mower for a long minute and finally shook his head. She wished she could see his face but immediately felt glad she couldn't.

At half past two in the morning, Jane took a break to survey her work. She had finished cleaning the house's interior until every room looked clean and neat. By moonlight the yard looked passable too. Mowing and raking may have taken the most time and effort, but they rendered the most noticeable results. She had managed to put some order into the shed that housed her reptiles and amphibians, just in case he looked in there. Her truck, now clean, fresh, and loaded with her small boat, collecting gear, and a dozen freshly laundered snake bags, sat ready for her adventure. The flower beds she had weeded didn't seem to need flowers after all. Nice, worked-up dirt definitely looked ornamental when not overgrown with weeds.

She grabbed the hose and sprayed the walk, washed the front door, and finally turned it on the windows. At that point, exhaustion convinced her that she should take him at his word and give him the real thing. A bag of peanut butter and jelly sandwiches and some bottles of water would have to suffice. After a quick shower, she crawled into bed and fell asleep instantly.

When the Lincoln slid silently into her drive at five-thirty, she had only been awake for fifteen minutes, but she had accomplished much in those minutes. She pretended not to know he had arrived and let him walk the entire length of her beautifully trimmed and washed front walk. That would give him time to notice the completely mowed yard and the spotless front door. She had worked hard for this minute and wanted to savor it. She had even unloaded a few items from her truck and piled them in her kitchen—as an excuse to have him step in and help carry. It was only right he should see how nice her house could look inside too.

"Good morning, Jane. Did you enjoy a good night's sleep?" He pushed open her door, not bothering to knock.

"Yes, plenty of sleep, and I'm ready for the day."

She found it difficult to hide her amusement when he stepped inside the brightly lit room. If Armani made a safari line, he wore it. He looked decidedly different from the Mr. Faircloth she had met yesterday. A khaki, short-sleeved shirt exposed well-muscled arms, while his legs, or the portion of them visible between khaki shorts and an obviously new pair of snake boots, were even more heavily muscled. Overall, he made a rather arresting picture, she decided. Finally, her eyes locked on a white scar directly below his knee that ran halfway around his leg.

"I'm not used to this much scrutiny," he announced, and she realized she had been staring.

"Oh, I was admiring your boots. Snake boots, aren't they?"

"They're supposed to be snake proof. Jane, you must curb this lying. It was the scar on my calf—not my boots—that caught your interest. And you couldn't have gotten more than two or three hours of sleep, if that long."

"Why would you think that? I . . ."

"Your walk is *quite* wet, and so is the front of your house—from when you obviously washed it a short while ago. I can actually guess how long it would take to mow a lot this size with a weed eater, weed a flower bed, and load a truck." He smiled challengingly at her. "Now, would you like to show me the rest of your nocturnal pursuits?"

"Just get in the truck, I'm ready."

She walked stormily into the kitchen to gather up the items she had stashed there, but he followed close behind and gathered them up before she had a chance.

"Weren't these in the back of your truck yesterday?"

"Yes, they were. I brought them in so you could admire my clean house when you came in to help me carry them back out."

"See how good it feels to tell the truth."

Murder again flitted lightly across her mind.

"You insinuated things about my housekeeping. You know—clean a room, even if the house is dirty. Isn't that what you said?"

"Why *Jane*, I merely referred to our publishing philosophy. I thought you'd be interested in the reputation of our company. You took it personally."

"You were looking around at my house."

"Old habit of mine. I always look around—at everything." His gaze grew uncomfortably piercing.

"You'll have plenty of chance for that today."

While she drove to the area chosen for that morning's work, she wondered what madness had possessed her to throw herself in the company of this overly inquisitive, totally unpredictable man. She refrained from conversation but secretly savored delicious thoughts of revenge. She was in *her* element now.

About ten miles from her house, she pulled off the highway into an opening that led to soybean fields. Familiar with the area, she knew there would be a series of fields, each with patches of woods, brush and blackberry briars surrounding them. Driving far enough off the road to hide her truck from passing drivers, she climbed out and hung her handwritten, *snake hunting* sign in the window.

"I use that in case the owner chances by and wonders who parked here. No one seems to mind it if I remove their snakes, but I have run into small patches of marijuana and other illicit situations at times. I don't want to make anyone nervous. Since I tramp a lot of miles, sometimes twenty or more in a day, I see all sorts of things."

The distance didn't astonish him like she had hoped it would. He seemed to take everything in stride. While he gazed off at the countryside, she slid a loose fitting, long sleeved cotton shirt over her long-sleeved turtleneck, strapped a sturdy leather belt around her waist, pulled a snagged, slightly unraveled, toboggan over her curls, and topped it all off with a faded, disreputable, cowboy hat. He suddenly turned around and looked at her astounded.

"I say now, for a minute I thought a street person had wandered over here to request a handout. Excuse me, Jane, but why the excessive clothing? It may be over one hundred degrees today."

"I would rather put up with the heat and have the extra protection from briars and mosquitoes. Mosquitoes can't usually sting through two layers of clothes. When I work in insect-infested swamp areas, I pull the toboggan down over my ears."

"Those don't look like snake boots."

"They're comfortable."

She hung half a dozen, thin cotton snake bags over her belt along with a bag of the peanut butter sandwiches she had prepared. When she saw he wore a canteen, she took only one of the plastic bottles of water and stuffed it into another bag on her belt. Finally, she deposited a length of nylon rope and a pocketknife into her pocket. His keen observation of all her proceedings discomfited her.

"Mr. Faircloth, I didn't bring any insect repellent. I don't generally use it. It's rather pricey, and I'm almost immune to chiggers since I've had so many bites. Mosquitoes can only get to my hands and face."

She felt gleeful and apologetic at the same time.

"That's quite all right, Jane." He opened a satchel on his belt and brought out a small vial of repellent. "I hadn't considered the terrain, or I'd have worn long pants. This type countryside is still new to me."

He acted nonchalant about everything. Nothing daunted this man. She had hoped to derive a measure of fun from a greenhorn, but now she wondered what kind of terrain he had expected—surely something much different from his meticulous office in Panama City. This man had the earmarks of someone who had done things, not someone who had only read about them.

"Explain the rake, Jane," he said as she brought a regular garden rake out of the back of her truck.

"This is my most useful tool. I use it to hold down snakes,

snare venomous snakes, vault small streams, and keep my balance when I cross wet areas on logs. When I walk across soggy ground, I use it like a cane with the rake head down. It helps to distribute my weight so I don't sink so deeply. I also use it to knock lizards out of trees, scoop snakes from the water, hold off mean dogs, and . . . and I have another one in the truck. Would you like to carry it?"

"Assuredly. I'm scared of mean dogs too."

The way he said it made her wonder if there was anything he *did* fear.

Reading her mind, he added, "I believe I'm frightened of *snakes* as well, and you may call me Reginald—or Reg."

"Not Reggie?"

"Not if you want me to sign that check."

She grinned and started around the field. He had pulled one on her. She didn't look back, but she could picture his smile. She would allow him his moment of victory because she knew she had the upper hand for at least this one day. He feared snakes. She had hoped for as much. Her fear of them had long ago passed. Now she felt only the exhilaration of the chase and reasonable respect for big rattlers and moccasins. When she trusted her face not to show any glee of anticipation, she turned to explain what would ensue.

Reginald had disappeared, but she heard crashing from the nearby trees. She rushed toward the sound and found Reginald climbing a small tree and shaking it vigorously as he proceeded upward.

"Reginald, what are you doing?"

"I used your *useful tool* to knock a lizard down, and now it's stuck in the tree."

"How would a lizard stick in a tree, or did you squash it against the tree? I can't use dead ones, you know."

"The blooming rake's stuck in the tree."

At that instant, he managed to shake it loose and catch it in midair as it tumbled toward the ground. His speedy descent from the tree resembled a plummet more than a calculated climb, but he seemed unaware or uninterested in the red abrasions on his legs. He stared wickedly at the rake as if it had failed him.

"How do you keep the rake from sticking in trees?'

"By holding onto it. I reach it up and rake a lizard out of the tree. If they travel too high, I leave and look for something else."

"What animals do we want besides snakes and lizards?"

"Skinks, small turtles, frogs, salamanders—almost any reptile or amphibian that moves on tree, land, or water except for protected species like box turtles or gopher turtles."

"I don't see any. Maybe I should go back and look for the lizard I lost."

"Come with me. Step as lightly as you can because these animals sense vibrations. Study the grass and weeds to your right—between the edge of the planted field and the tree line. You're searching for a different color or movement or the sound of movement. Early in the morning, snakes often lie at the edge of fields to enjoy the sun or wait for prey."

She stayed to his left, rather than in front, anxious for him to make a catch. When she espied the first snake, a racer, she tried to contain her impatience and pretend she didn't see it. Right away he noticed her lighter, more cautious step.

"What do you see? Ah, I see him. Maybe you should try for him. I'd hate to lose him for you."

"You go for it. Approach it cautiously and lightly. If it starts to move, rush it. Put the rake down on it quickly—but gently."

"Am I supposed to pin its head?"

"Pin it anywhere on its body. Aim for its middle."

"It's not venomous, is it?" He still hesitated.

"No. Just a racer."

That instant the snake moved. Reginald charged it, brought the rake down on it swiftly, but gingerly, and stood amazed as it slithered away from under his rake.

Jane ran forward and put the toe of her boot lightly on its body before it could disappear into the brush.

"Didn't I push hard enough? I didn't want to kill it."

"My fault. I forgot to tell you not to use the prong side. You use the flat side of the rake head. We don't want to skewer them. We need them alive."

"I wondered about that. I tried to aim between the prongs. Now what do we do?"

"How much do you want to do?"

"Assuredly not touch the confounded thing."

"Okay. Hold this bag open. When I put the snake in, you close the top. You can watch how I do it."

She took the snake by the tail, swung the rest of its body between her legs, and tightened her thighs against it. When she pulled it back through, she grasped its head firmly as soon as it appeared.

"See its mouth?" she explained as Reginald backed away two steps. "Those sharp little teeth can draw blood but don't hurt much if they bite you."

"Didn't it bite the backs of your legs?"

"Snakes don't usually bite through two layers of pants. I wear long johns under my jeans. Water snakes sometimes bite through, though. Their teeth resemble razors, which helps them handle their diet of fish. They'll give you a worse bite because they slice you. I have some small scars on my hands from past mishaps."

"Bloody well glad I wore shorts."

"Why?"

"Because you won't expect me to pick up any snakes."

"There are many other ways to do it."

"Put it in the bag, Jane." He held the open bag at arm's length.

She had hardly lowered the snake into the depths of the bag when he violently closed it on her wrist.

"Ouch! Reginald, you're supposed to let me get my hand out before you close it." She pried off his clenched fists.

"I'm sorry. I was afraid it would get away or . . . or get to me. Did I hurt you?"

"You have good reflexes anyway."

"How much money did we make?"

"A dollar."

"A dollar? That's all they pay you to risk your life? No wonder you need expenses."

"Some snakes bring in as much as twenty dollars or even more. I'm paid by the foot for most snakes. I earn fifty cents a foot for water snakes, a dollar a foot for gray rat snakes, two dollars for red rats, three for king snakes, and four or four-fifty a foot for diamondbacks, but a racer is only worth a buck no matter its size.

I sell mostly to wholesalers, and they don't pay much, but I need to photograph specimens for my book, so the money is just a bonus."

"Oh, indeed. But in my office yesterday you intimated you *lived* on that money. How can you call it a bonus? It sounds exceedingly important. Surely, with your zoology degree you could make satisfactory money—better than this anyway. You could do most of your photography at reptile parks and save all this trouble and risk."

For an instant her mind went blank. When it functioned again, she felt her face grow hot. In the query letter she sent to him at his London publishing house, she had mentioned she studied zoology in college, but she never mentioned a *degree*. She had only wanted him to realize her qualifications to write the book. Now what would this product of Oxford think if he knew she hadn't finished college? Would he change his mind about the book? It *was* a scientific book, and she owned no credentials. Everyone expected credentials. Confound that query letter. Why did he have to remember that?

"Jane, why are you mutilating the ground with your rake? Is there some kind of small beastie we have to dig out of the dirt?"

She lifted her eyes in one swift defiant look.

"I don't have a zoology degree. I left college . . . early."

Mentally she kissed her nature books goodbye. He watched her intently, as if he expected her to say more, and a feeling of recklessness swept over her.

"I was working my way through college. When my expenses increased and my job disintegrated, I quit school so I could collect and write full time."

"Oh, come now, Jane. You don't seem like the type who'd quit over a wee lack of money. Of course you could find another job."

"I didn't *want* another job. My science professor told me about this collecting work because he thought it might help me pay my expenses. You can't imagine how wonderful it felt to get outdoors in the sun and the weather. I couldn't go back to the drudgery. My spirit rebelled."

"Does it do that often? Are there any danger signals I should watch for? Besides your eyes, that is?"

She grew self-conscious and could no longer meet his gaze, which seemed to bore through her. She grabbed her rake and began walking. They soon came to a secluded nook in the woods where they startled some wild turkeys into flight. Jane stepped back under the trees and found a small stream flowing through it.

"I'll leave our lunch here in this shady spot, and we can eat on our way back." After she had taken a drink from her water bottle, she left it submerged in the cool water and attached their sandwich bag to the end of a low tree limb. "I don't like to have too much hanging on my belt. The reptiles can get weighty if I have good luck."

"Do you ever drink the water in these tiny streams?"

"Have you noticed all the chemical bags and containers around these fields—not always empty containers either. When it rains, the runoff water carries chemicals from all those bags as well as the chemicals used on the ground and vegetation into these little streams. That's enough to discourage me from drinking runoff water."

He took a swallow from his thermos. "How about our sandwiches? Won't some bug or the heat ruin them?"

"I brought peanut butter and jelly sandwiches, a safer choice for warm temperatures. We may find a few ants on the bag by the time we get back, but not much worse can happen."

They had gone halfway around the next field when Reginald stopped abruptly and pointed at a tall tree.

"Jane, look at that big lizard on that tree. It has a red head."

"That's a broad-headed skink. They're difficult to catch. That one's gone too far up the tree to rake . . ."

He dropped his rake, ran three steps, and leaped, snatching it off the tree trunk before she could finish her sentence. He landed solidly back on his feet with a jubilant expression on his face—until it bit him.

"This one isn't venomous either, right?" He held the eight inches of squirming, brown plumpness at arm's length.

"It's harmless. Here, drop it in this bag."

"It won't let go. What a big mouth it has. How do I get it to open its mouth?

She gently opened its jaw and it dropped into her bag. For a few seconds Reginald studied his bleeding finger with interest, but before she had put the bag back on her belt, he had started hunting again. She caught up with him and matched her steps to his.

During the next couple of hours, he caught a number of lizards and skinks, and though he spotted one snake, he insisted she capture and bag it. He had accumulated a number of abrasions, and his shirt was wet and torn, but he looked pleased. He stopped, took off his hat, and looked around him.

"This jaunt has exceeded my expectations. I continue to find this entire panhandle area intriguing."

"What brought you here in the beginning? This locale isn't some international tourist spot, except for kids on spring break, and it's a long way from home for you."

Minutes passed as they walked silently. She had already decided he wasn't going to answer when finally she heard him draw a deep breath.

"Anna brought me here."

"Your secretary? The one I met in your office?"

"Her husband, John, belonged to the 48th Fighter Wing—stationed near London. I met him and Anna when our publishing house did a book on the 48th." He stopped walking and stared out at the woods. "When John's tour of duty ended, he accompanied me on a business trip—of sorts. He and Anna both considered it a good opportunity for him to make a small nest egg and finance his return to civilian life. She flew home to be with her family here in Panama City, and he planned to follow in about a month. As it turned out, it *wasn't* a good opportunity, not for John anyway. He was . . . he died, and I flew over here to do what I could for Anna as soon as I could."

"And you fell in love with this area?" Jane asked softly, remembering how the article about him had mentioned that he fell under the spell of Florida.

"Yes." He smiled at her and seemed to throw off his somber mood. "I liked the climate, the Gulf, and the miles and miles of unimproved countryside. When I found a publishing company that needed a new owner, I grabbed the opportunity. I'd always intended to start a branch operation of our London firm in the United States. It was my chance to do my own thing." Enthusiasm had returned to his voice.

"But I read that your father retired and left you the London firm? How can you run both places?"

"The London office employs enough vastly qualified, old-timers to keep things going. I can easily run it from here or fly back if I'm needed. Dad still dabbles too."

"Has he been retired for long?"

"Not long. He waited until I culminated a small project out of the country."

"Starting this new publishing house here? Doing your own thing?"

"Not *here*. Not *this* project. I was in Zaire investigating . . ." He paused and grinned sheepishly. "Doing my own thing."

"See. I'm not the only one whose spirit rebels."

"But *I* finished school first." He smiled annoyingly.

Jane gave him her best withering glance and continued around the field. She thought she heard a low chuckle behind her. Presently he walked by her side again, totally involved in the work at hand, but he had aroused Jane's curiosity. What had he started to say about Zaire before he clammed up? She would have questioned him further if he hadn't gone back to the subject of education. At least it appeared she was still an employed writer, in spite of her lack of a degree.

By the time they returned to the spot where they had left their lunch, her bags had grown heavy with specimens. The morning's work produced a rat snake, two racers, a green tree snake, and assorted skinks and lizards, which Reginald had grown adept at catching.

"I do believe it's easier to capture them if you don't let them see your eyes," Reginald said as they sat on a log and ate their sandwiches.

"I've always thought so too. I'm surprised you noticed that."

"Look over there, Jane. What luck. We get to add one more snake to our collection."

"Go ahead—collect it."

Jane anticipated some real fun as Reginald rushed forward, rake poised for the capture. The snake raised and flattened its head like a cobra and hissed viciously at him. He nervously stepped back a few steps.

"It looks poisonous."

"Drag it over closer. Don't let it get away in the brush. That's a good-sized hognose snake, over three feet long. It has an excellent skin design too. I'll use it for a photo in my book."

"I don't think it likes me. Uh-oh. You won't photograph this one. I believe I've crushed it."

The snake appeared to have died in a spasm of pain. It lay on its back with its jaw twisted open in a lopsided contortion of agony. Its tongue drooped out one side of its mouth.

Jane kept a straight face as she picked the snake up by the middle of its body. It hung limply. She wore her most hopeless expression.

"I say now, Jane, I didn't pin it *that* violently. I pressed the rake down quite gently. Maybe the blooming snake was already sick or injured."

Jane stretched the snake out on the grass. With a firm hold on its tail, she turned the snake over. Almost quicker than eye could see, it returned to its back, its mouth still agape in a grotesque position. Jane turned it a few more times, with the same result each time. Reginald became curious and got on his knees beside it. With a piece of stick, he turned it over, but it always ended up on its back.

"Let's wait a few minutes and watch," Jane suggested.

After about five minutes the snake somehow ended up on its belly and slid off into the grass. Jane ran and grabbed it. Immediately it became a dead snake again.

"Well, by Jove."

"Isn't *by Jove* sort of an antiquated expression—I mean, like even in England? I didn't know anyone still used that expression."

"I do." His voice definitely reprimanded, but his gaze never left the drama in the grass. "It's pretending. I never hurt it at all. It's playing opossum."

"They sometimes do that when they're scared. This one would make a good pet. It will mainly feed on toads."

"Do you catch toads too?"

"They're worth a nickel apiece. I get them at night with a light."

"Don't sell that snake just yet. I may want to buy it from you."

"Of course. Would you like to hold it?"

"Put it in the bag, Jane, and hang it on your belt with the rest of the critters. I'll carry your water bottle. By the way, you don't hang rattlesnakes on your belt, do you?"

"Hardly. They'd strike through the bag. I hang the bag on the end of my rake and carry it over my shoulder. I could carry the bag by hand if I held it above the knot, but I might get careless and swing it against my leg."

"Have you ever been careless? I mean, have you ever been bitten by a venomous snake?"

"Careless? Yes. Bitten? No. I did almost sit on one of my bagged rattlesnakes, but he obligingly warned me before he struck."

"By Jove. A bite there would be bloody embarrass—"

"Never mind," she quickly interrupted. "It didn't happen. Let's get back to my truck and drive to Wrights Creek now."

Chapter 3

*Eighty dollars equal eighty dollars—
in English and in broken English.*

"We'll collect here this afternoon. I'm glad you brought other shoes for our boat trip."

Jane felt real misgivings when she pulled the weighty, seven-foot boat from the back of her truck. It looked small, terribly small, for two people, and its faded fluorescent-orange plastic hull embarrassed her for the first time.

"This is a boat, right? These gaping crevices on the bottom that run from end to end don't mean anything—correct?" he asked as he lifted one side of the boat and helped carry it to the water's edge.

"It's full of flotation, so it won't sink. I just draws a little water. That makes it slightly cumbersome, but the current isn't strong in the creek. We'll float with the current and row back."

"These couldn't possibly serve for oars, could they? This one looks like a piece of tin screwed to a piece of wood?" He picked up one of the oars and turned it over in his hands as he studied it curiously.

"I made them myself."

"Somehow I knew you would say that."

"I know they look a trifle rough, but they work."

"And where will we end up if they don't?"

"The Choctawhatchee River, first, and then eventually the Gulf of Mexico. I've wanted to take that trip someday."

"You didn't make the boat too, did you?"

"You could call it a gift—sort of. My neighbors tossed it out, and there was a lot of good life left in it."

"I'd hate to see your idea of a dead boat. Promise you'll not throw any live snakes into this wee boat."

He hesitated, one foot in and one foot out, while he waited for her answer.

"I promise, but if one drops off a tree limb, don't blame me. You do swim, don't you?"

"Like a fish, but I didn't dress for swimming today." He shoved the boat off and picked up one of the oars.

"The creeks still in flood from the last rain. There will be quite a few branches leaning over the water, and that's where we'll find turtles and snakes. See the small turtles on that stump ahead of us? I'll send the boat there as quickly as possible. You be ready to snatch any you can. They'll probably all jump before we get there."

When the boat approached, four little turtles plopped into the water. Jane caught nothing, but Reginald plunged his arm into the dark water and came up with a two-inch slider.

"Great. Put it in that bag, and we'll try for that water snake over there in the crotch of that tree. I'll try to grab it if you can send the boat in that direction. If it drops into the water, forget it."

"What's the best way to make it drop into the water?"

"Reginald!"

"Okay, Nature Girl. Get ready."

"Too late, it's gone.

"Is that a snake stretched out on that tree branch? On the right, about fifty yards."

"Two water snakes."

The smaller one dropped into the water as they approached, but the other one awoke too late, and she grabbed it.

"A tidy job, Jane. You keep the snake bags at your end, and I'll take care of the turtle bags, okay?"

After a number of near misses, they came to an area where the creek widened. A submerged island of cypress trees stood in the center with only the tops of the trees standing out of the water.

"See it?" Jane pointed toward a nearby tree. "Back in the

branches? Can you paddle us there bow first? Try not to brush against any limbs or the snake will feel it. It's a tight squeeze, but I think the boat will fit."

Jane leaned far out over the bow, ducked the low hanging limbs, and snatched the snake as it slid into the water. When she turned to show it to Reginald, he had disappeared. She stared, unbelieving, at the contents of the small boat, but it contained nothing larger than a turtle bag. At that second, she saw his hat bobbing in the current as if trying to make an escape. She paddled furiously toward it as if she expected to find him under it. She scooped it out and ducked her face into the water to see if Reginald had sunk into the depths below, but she could only see a few inches into the dark water.

She worked herself into a state of panic. Had she drowned her publisher? In a frantic attempt to see deeper into the water, she leaned far out over the side of the boat.

"Jane. Over here."

Completely started by his voice, she plunged head first into the water. When she resurfaced, she located him in the middle of the creek. His head and one arm were above the surface of the water, and he waved at her.

They both reached the boat at about the same time, though he shoved her aboard before he climbed in.

"I'm sorry, Reg," she sputtered. "I didn't know you weren't in the boat with me."

"I leaned over the side when we passed under a branch. I didn't want to brush it and scare your snake away. Next thing I knew, I was in the water—as neat as that."

"This boat doesn't rock much from side to side, so I didn't feel any movement when you decided to swim. And believe me, I understand exactly how you managed to plunge into the water—now. We can mop up a little with some of these empty snake bags. Anything on you that water will ruin?"

"My pride."

"Would you like to go back now? We've had a rather full day."

"Go back when it's just becoming fun? I like it back here. This is a rather primeval place."

"You'd definitely love it if we floated all the way to the

Choctawhatchee. I always find primeval spots along that river.

"I know somewhat about that locale. I own two parcels of acreage on that river, about halfway between here and Panama City. I've never stepped foot on either of them, just viewed them from the highway, but they looked rather wild and grown over. Would they be a good place to hunt reptiles?"

"Possibly, if no one's been on them for a while."

"Let's go there in the morning and call it a day now. I know you didn't get any sleep last night, and I have a pressing concern at the office that I need to investigate further. Let's get you home or Cootie will be angry with me." He grinned knowingly.

"It's *Cody*." She started to say more but bit her tongue.

On the drive back she somehow lost the free, easy feeling she had enjoyed earlier. The sudden mention of Cody had sobered her. She almost felt guilty over how enjoyable the day had been. She had let herself go. The out-of-doors always released something in her. Now she was embarrassed at how personal and chummy she had been. Had she overstepped? The cab of the truck suddenly shrank, and he became her publisher again, and a stranger. She couldn't think of anything to say. When he finally spoke, she was relieved to have the silence broken.

"Jane, you said you weren't at home much. Is it because of work on the book? Photography? Field research?"

"Yes. I'm trying to cover every type of terrain and climate in Florida—from the Keys to the Alabama line. I also do programs for schools. I've lined up a number of schools where I exhibit my reptiles and educate the students about them. That gives me a few extra bucks and helps pay expenses while I work in different areas of the state."

"Why do you keep turning that ring round and round? Is it uncomfortable? A poor fit?"

"I didn't realize I was. I'm not used to wearing much jewelry."

"It hasn't been on that finger for long then? The finger does seem to be rebelling. Maybe it expected something slightly more . . . elegant? You'll rub all the paint off if you don't stop fussing with it."

"I think it's a lovely ring." She spread her fingers wide and examined it without looking his way. "A *very* lovely ring," she repeated with more enthusiasm than she felt.

"I always thought a gift such as that, something that means so much, should be something more lasting." The mocking tone in his voice maddened her.

"Well, I always thought the best gifts were often the most perishable, you know, something that's greatly enjoyed and leaves a pleasant memory. Memories last longer and mean more than most material items. I often make up fancy baskets of fruit when gift-giving occasions arise. Most of the people I know have too much of the material anyway. I couldn't afford to give a lasting gift of that type, one that they'd actually appreciate, so I opt for a memory instead."

"That's quite commendable, Jane. And for your sake, I hope it lasts longer than a basket of fruit, or that you at least get a good memory from it."

She glared at him out of the corner of her eye and saw that he smiled again. She should shove him onto the highway or take him back to the creek and drown him. Maybe she should drop a snake down his boot. A dozen such appropriate tortures had flitted through her mind by the time she finally pulled into her drive.

"Let me help you put things away," he said and started to pull the boat from the back of the truck.

"That's not necessary. You need to get back, and I always do it myself."

"Of course it's necessary. What do you think I am? You carry the snakes though."

Much to Jane's exasperation, Reginald helped until she had put the last reptile away in its *critter hotel*—as he had dubbed the reptile shed behind her house. When it became obvious that he looked around for something else to do, she grew uneasy.

"Would you like a cold drink before you go? Lemonade? Some iced tea?"

He studied her for a second. "I need to push on. I'll be back here at five in the morning. We'll go in my car. Promise you'll sleep?"

"Immediately."

"Wash your hands first. They smell of snake."

Jane awoke next morning with new excitement. She had almost forgiven Reginald's former trespasses and actually looked forward to the day ahead. Not only would it be interesting to explore the river in a new spot, but her evening held promise too. It was Cody's weekend to come home from New Orleans, and they would go out that night. She told herself that Cody caused her light, happy feeling, but knew she wasn't being totally honest. More and more, doubts had sprung up regarding their relationship. Tonight maybe she could dispel them.

She stared into her coffee cup and was deep in thought when Reginald arrived—early. It both amused and nettled her when he loaded her collecting paraphernalia into his car as if it was his responsibility. No one had ever taken over that way, and she sighed resignedly.

Stiffly perched on the luxurious seat, she took great care to keep her ring hand out of sight. She would avoid any verbal battles regarding Cody, regarding *anything*, and she wouldn't indulge in any more psychological word games with him if she could help it. They soon came to a halt along the empty stretch of highway.

"Jane, the old logging trail enters here. It marks the beginning of my property. It's not driveable, but maybe we can at least get off the road here at its start."

"Not with that huge log there."

"That's a new addition. It wasn't here when the owner brought me to see this place. I know, because we parked precisely in that spot while we went over his plats and papers."

"Maybe the owner put it there after you purchased the property—to keep people off."

"He couldn't have stepped over it, much less moved it, and I've driven past here a number of times. It's definitely a brand new addition. Wait here and I'll see if I can get in there."

He walked a short distance and cleared the area of dead limbs. When he hefted the log and moved it easily to one side, she began to wonder about this man. There was more to him than met the eye. She watched his easy stride as he returned. He definitely hadn't spent all his life behind a desk.

"The path looks navigable for about twenty yards. Let's drive in a ways so no one's tempted to break into my car."

"You said you had two parcels of land. Do they adjoin?"

"No, the other is about half a mile south of here." He opened out an aerial picture of the area and studied it closely. "They both front on this highway and run all the way back to the river. I don't know who owns the tract in between. I'd like to look at both my purchases if we have the time."

"We'll have to proceed more cautiously here than around plowed fields," Jane said as she surveyed the heavy undergrowth. Pine tops and branches lay everywhere, brown corpses peeking out of the almost chest-high tangle of weeds. "I can barely make out the trail. We won't be able to see what's around our feet most of the time. We'll have to walk slow and carefully."

They had gone only a short distance when Jane abruptly took off at a full run. After about ten yards, she stopped, turned sharply, and ran in a different direction. Covering about fifteen feet in that direction, she jumped, reversed again, and headed off on a new course.

"I say, Jane, has the sun gotten to you?"

When Reginald caught up with her, she continued to run back and forth as if she were mentally deranged.

Swiftly she plunged the rake down and grabbed a long snake of an unusual light brown hue. She sat on the ground, panting, and looked over her prize.

"I thought you'd gone daft on me or were performing some ritual to the snake gods. Don't scare me like that." His face looked a study of concern and wonder.

"He kept ch-charging me." She gasped and tried to catch her breath. "J-Just when I'd almost c-catch up with him, he'd go between my legs and head off in a new direction. I wasn't sure which of us would wear out first. It's a coach whip—almost seven feet long. What a beauty."

"It's a snake, Jane. I see beauty in many places, but . . ."

"It's a *beautiful* snake." She rose abruptly, bagged the snake, and hung it on her belt. "This is a rather beautiful piece of land, too. You own all of this property?"

"Everything south of this trail. This trail passes along its northern boundary. When we hit the river, we follow it south until we come to a small stream, possibly a dry streambed. That marks the southern boundary. The other tract has a stream marking its southern boundary too, according to the maps I have on it."

"Your trail just disappeared. You have swamp between the river and us. I don't know how wide it is. Do you want to go through it or skirt the edge of it for a while?"

"It's early. Let's keep our feet dry as long as we can."

"All right, but it looks crossable. If it doesn't get any deeper, it could probably be crossed without having to wade."

"Do you swing on giant grape vines, or is it some other trick that only professional snake nabbers know?"

She studied his face. He held his mouth shut firmly—but his eyes definitely laughed at her.

"It's not any accomplishment worth mentioning," she said dubiously. "But when you walk in the woods as much as I do, you learn whether something will hold your weight, whether it's really as solid as it appears. It's instinctive, I guess. You know where to put your feet."

"Maybe I should follow you. I never know where to put my feet—and Anna tells me I often put them in my mouth."

Jane's smile showed she agreed wholeheartedly with his secretary, but she kept her eyes intently on the path.

"There's a narrow strip of higher ground here that might take us through the swamp, maybe all the way to the river. Watch close for snakes. This is a good place for a rattler or moccasin to sun."

Around the next curve, they came unexpectedly upon a cultivated meadow of small plants.

"Marijuana." Jane said in surprise.

A man jumped up from his resting spot under a tree and looked ready to run off. Jane's immediate inclination was to do the same, only in a different direction. Reginald had no such propensity. He walked calmly up to him.

"I say there, young man, I'm Reginald Faircloth. Why are you planting marijuana here on my property?"

From his businesslike tone, Reginald could have been at his mahogany desk in his plush office. The other man, who couldn't have been more than seventeen or eighteen, hesitated when Reginald addressed him. He wore no shirt, and his tan, clean-shaven face registered as much alarm as Jane felt. Suddenly he lost his frightened look and smiled broadly.

"Ah, Mr. Faircloth! I José. I glad for meet you. This best place, why we plant here." His sweeping gesture proudly indicated the field of marijuana. "Good soil. Airplane no see easy. Far back you place. No people see. Swamp all around."

"A blooming patch of marijuana? On my Land?"

Jane could see that Reginald had started to lose it.

"No bloom. Seedlings. Bloom later. We plant big patch on you place over there. Seedlings too." He motioned toward the south, obviously meaning Reginald's other tract of land. "Lubin find two more good places for to plant. You get big crop. Lubin and Tomás go get fertilize."

His gestures and animated face showed his excitement and pleasure at meeting Reginald. Jane tried to understand the situation. She noted the bewildered look on Reginald's face and grasped he was as stupefied as she was. For once he was at a loss for words. He obviously knew nothing of the marijuana or of this José. She nervously jumped in with the only thoughts that would come to her mind.

"Good work, José. Are you all by yourself here? When will Lu . . . Lubin and Tomás be back?"

"Not soon. Hours. Maybe two, three hours."

"They're careful where they park, aren't they?" she ventured, remembering that Reginald had parked his shiny car only a short distance off the road. What would happen if they came back and saw it?

"Park long way at bridge. Use boat. We get more seedlings soon, when Mr. Webb bring more money." He turned his attention back to Reginald. "He say you give money to him, he bring Sunday. He come see fields Sunday. You bring money now?"

A wave of comprehension rolled over Reginald's face as he came alive to the situation.

"No. I came to check on . . ." Jane could tell he struggled to say something that sounded sensible. Then a light of inspiration shone in his eyes. "I came to check on Mr. Webb, to make sure he doesn't cheat me. What time will he meet you on Sunday? Will he meet you here?"

"He come Sunday night. Meet at shed." He motioned in the

direction of the other parcel of land.

"Is that where you planted the other patch?"

"Sí. You want I show?" José asked eagerly with a friendly, trusting smile.

"I'll check it later. Who's in charge here?"

"Most Lubin. He uncle to me. Tomás is brother. I hoe, plant." He sighed and shrugged.

Reginald either didn't sense the risk or didn't care. Jane began to think it was the latter. She was getting used to Reginald's ways. His usual inquisitiveness had asserted itself. Obviously he wanted to understand the situation better, but Jane thought it was past time to leave.

"Do you like the work, José?" Reginald continued conversationally while Jane desperately tugged at the back of his shirt to get him out of there.

"No like much. Hot, no friends, and much bugs. But money much good. I tell Lubin and Tomás you come. You want meet?"

"Certainly, I . . ."

Jane quickly interrupted. "No. Not now. We can't stay. We only want to talk with *you*, José. We don't want Mr. Webb to know we've checked on him." She wanted to kick Reginald in the ankle before he got them into real trouble.

"José, would you like to work for me?" Reginald asked, taking the ball again. "I need someone to watch things for me, to keep their eyes and ears open. You can't tell *anyone* I was here because they could accidentally let it slip out. Do this job for me, and I'll pay you extra—later on. You seem like a keen bloke."

"Sí, I clean broke. Need money. I spy much good. Gracias."

"One more thing, José. You should use more caution. What if I was a policeman? How do you know I'm Mr. Faircloth? I could have lied."

"I much careful. Mr. Webb, he show pictures. He want we know Mr. Faircloth. He say you maybe come."

"I always come, José, but I never tell him."

He winked, and José laughed. Reginald's off-hand manner had gained much information, and José's intent, clear eyes already showed admiration for Reginald.

"Sí, *I* think you smart man. *Lubin* say you no smart. He want you send cash, no send check. He say check no smart. Cash smart."

It took Reginald a minute to assimilate that new piece of information, but he finally responded with a plausible enough explanation.

"I use checks so Webb can't cheat you. He might try to keep some. How much was the last check? I've forgotten. Did I send enough?" Reginald risked asking.

Jane held her breath and waited to see if a question like that would make José suspicious.

"Five hundred. Lubin go bank."

"Any trouble?"

"No trouble. He do like Mr. Webb say. No trouble."

José paused and looked thoughtful. He studied Reginald's face carefully. The boy might be inexperienced, but he was quick and bright.

"Mr. Faircloth, I no tell Lubin you come, but you prove you Mr. Faircloth. I no want trouble if maybe Lubin find out."

"Now I'm certain you're the right man for this job, José. I like cautious people." He pulled out his driver's license and showed it to José.

"Gracias. Thank you." José examined it closely, following across it with his fingertip.

"Do you read English?" Reginald finally asked when José continued his scrutiny.

"Yes. I read not good. I read name—Ra-ge-nald Fair-cloth."

"You should work on your reading, José. There's not much future in Marijuana. Have you been here long? In the United States, I mean."

"No here long. Long time Mexico. But I United States citizen. Have license for drive car. Have referencia letter for job." He produced said documents from deep in a front pocket. Reginald accepted them and handed José's license to Jane while he examined the ragged, much folded letter.

Reginald looked up at José with an exasperated mien. "José, this letter's written in Spanish."

"*Sí.* You no read Spanish good?"

"I no rea—I *don't* read Spanish at all. I *believe* I read English well enough to get by though."

Reginald didn't try to hide his discomfiture when he handed the letter back to José.

"I read letter you. I read Spanish much good."

"Never mind."

Jane could have laughed at the look on Reginald's face. José had one on him. *He* could read *two* languages. She smiled at José and handed back the driver's license. It looked authentic. She had memorized his address, noting it was in a small migrant community in south Florida.

"If I gave you money now, would Lubin or Tomás find out?" Reginald asked and brought out his wallet.

"I hide money. I save. Save for car."

Jane watched as Reginald started to bring out a five-dollar bill. She took the wallet from him, peeled off four twenties from the healthy wad of bills, and stuffed them into Reginald's hand with a meaningful look. Reginald looked astonished but handed the bills to José.

"You watch and let me know everything you hear. And be more careful. Don't fall asleep back here. The wrong person could catch you. Handle this right, and I'll pay you more money."

"Sí. Gracias." José tucked the money into his letter and returned it to his pocket.

On their walk back to the car, Reginald complained, "For someone who spends all day gathering snakes that bring a buck apiece, you were awfully generous with my money. I guess I'd better warn this Cootie fellow what he's getting into."

"It's *Cody*," she corrected. "And the marijuana work José's involved with pays better than a five spot. Even migrant work pays better than that. He may not speak good English, but that doesn't mean he can't tell a twenty from a five."

"Five dollars seemed quite generous."

"He's a farmer, not a writer, Reg," she replied, copping his own phrase.

"Here, take my keys and back the car out while I put things back like they were. We don't want anyone else to know we've been here. *Maybe* José won't tell."

He repositioned the log and hurriedly climbed in to take over the driving.

"We'd best head back."

"Don't you want to check on your other crops? Nice hobby you have, Reginald."

"I'll check—but I'll take you home first." His stern frown showed he felt more concern than he let on.

"And let me miss all the fun? Are you afraid I'll turn you in?"

"I'm afraid if I run into more farmers, you won't leave me enough money for lunch. . . . Now don't laugh, Jane. It isn't funny."

"I know, but listen. I've run into marijuana before, though on a much smaller basis. I think, no, I *know* I can walk more silently than you can. Besides, you promised to take me to the river. We'd better hurry though."

He studied her face for a moment. "Okay. But let's park somewhere on the other side of the road. Look at this aerial of the tract and find the best route for walking in."

"What's this—a building of sorts?" She pointed to a small structure in the picture, barely visible in the surrounding foliage. "That's the shed he mentioned, isn't it?"

"Probably. I figured that was what he meant."

"It's close to the river. I make out a couple of open areas near it. They probably planted the marijuana in one of those. There's a line of swamp, like on your other property, between them and the shed. Here's a faint line. It might be another logging road. It fades out before in gets to the shed. The stream on the south side of your land runs into the river and it runs back under this highway too. Have you crossed any sort of bridge?"

"Just did." He stopped and backed up. "This must be it. Let's find a place to park."

About a quarter of a mile ahead, they found a place to pull into. With the car well out of sight, they hurried back to the bridge that marked the second tract. It didn't take long to find the logging trail.

"It looks like this trail has a complimentary log also. Probably the work of my farmers."

"I guess we'd better walk quietly and quickly."

He looked at her amusedly.

The logging trail wore as much undergrowth as the other trail. It ended abruptly at the swamp's edge, but they found a narrow path leading through a less swampy area. Fresh footprints still showed in the soft muck.

"Try to step where you won't leave any new tracks," Jane advised as she treaded only on cypress knees and chunks of rotted wood. Reginald followed suit and shortly they came to higher ground. The shed stood there in its rickety splendor. It wasn't much more than an old plywood box, about eight feet wide by sixteen feet long, with a rusted tin roof and partially rotted plywood floor. There were no window openings, but light beamed through holes in the tin and through the narrow door opening, which no longer sported a door. The missing door, with bent rusty hinges still attached, lay warped and rotting in a pile of debris.

"Look, Jane. Grains of fertilizer. They probably store it in here. Let's see where they pull up the boat."

"It looks like they bring it into these reeds. That would hide it from view. I think we should check your crop and get out of here." "Jane, you keep saying it's my crop. You don't believe . . ."

"Of course not. You're face shows everything. And since you're so candid, I'm sure you'd tell me if you grew marijuana."

"I'm sure I wouldn't, but I don't. Now I have to find out what's going on."

"Do you have any enemies? I mean *real* enemies."

"Dozens. I step on toes all the time—both in my publishing and elsewhere. But it couldn't be something like that."

"It would *have* to be something like that. There's wilderness all over the state, secluded, hard to get to places. If someone wants to grow marijuana, those places are available for the finding. No need for someone to seek out a particular owner and perpetrate a hoax like this. Not only were these men given your name, Reginald, they were shown pictures of you. You'd better see if you've written any five hundred dollar checks recently. By the way, who's Mr. Webb?"

"Beats me, but I'm anxious to meet him."

Jane shivered at the ominous ring of his words. Abruptly, they came upon a large open area.

"Well, here's my crop. They're only babies. Look a mite sickly, don't you think?"

"Newly planted. They'll spruce up with rain and fertilizer. I think we'd better hurry out of here. Let's cut across. That trail we came in on makes me nervous."

They made their own zigzag trail back toward the highway, picking the clearest terrain. For a while they skirted the swamp, which began to deepen and finally became a small lake. Without warning a loud sound like a gunshot sent them both to their knees in the grass. Reginald pushed her lower when the sound repeated itself near the other end of the lake. Jane started to laugh uncontrollably.

"Jane, have you cracked on me," he shook her by the shoulders with grave concern on his face."

"It's beavers," she said, trying to restrain herself. "They heard us coming and smacked their tails on the water to warn the others. They *made* this lake. It's not in your picture."

"Blasted beavers. They gave me a good bit of a startle. I felt sure I'd gotten you into a terrible pickle with people shooting at us. As it stands now, I've made a bloody mess of things, getting you mixed up in this matter."

Jane began to wonder if this man knew fear at all. He didn't register fright in the same way most people did. He had only been anxious on her account. If she hadn't been with him, he probably would have waited back there with José and introduced himself to Lubin and Tomás. She could almost hear him say, "Hello, I'm Reginald Faircloth. Which one of you chaps is Lubin?"

"It's a pleasant lake they've built," she said, disconcerted by his solicitous study of her. "I often see beavers when I tramp near the water. See. There's one swimming over there. That's their den in the middle of the lake. If we follow on around, we'll probably find their dam. I like beavers, but around here they're considered nuisances because they flood areas—destroy a lot of trees. Consequently, they're often destroyed by irate landowners."

"I understand the problem, but couldn't they be trapped and moved to a new location? I know that's done with quite a few animals."

"It would be difficult. I've live-trapped a number of mammal species in my collecting work. Not only are beavers difficult to trap that way, but there's another consideration. Beavers mate for life. I wouldn't want to trap one unless I also captured its mate. I'd hate to think I sentenced one to a lonely life without its lifelong playmate and partner."

"I didn't know there were animals like that. They *have* something on us, don't they? They've made a rather scenic spot back here. It reminds me of another place I spent some time in once. Guess we'll have to go around it if we want to get out. This is nice, Jane. I've needed a break like this. Been behind a desk too much lately."

Was he even worried about this new situation, she wondered as they struggled through denser foliage and brush. Ever aware of her surroundings, a few minutes later she spotted a five-foot diamondback coiled at the edge of a blackberry patch.

"Whoa, Reginald, don't move."

"What?"

"A diamondback. It's on the move. Wait here." She plunged into the briar patch after it, though the sharp, clinging thorns slowed her progress. "It's getting away."

"No. It turned. I see it. It's headed toward you. Get out of there, Jane."

Finding it impossible to use her rake in the thick briars, she had no choice but to heed Reginald's advice. Keeping the snake in view, she backed out as quickly as she could. When the clinging blackberries caused her to almost fall on top of the snake, she heard Reginald's sharp gasp somewhere close by. She managed to plunge out of the briars in time to see the snake heading back into the brush in a new spot. Only its tail remained visible, and that was what she grabbed.

"I'm not going to lose this one. It's worth over twenty dollars."

With both hands, she pulled hard on the tail to drag it out of the briars. She had dragged it halfway out when the rattle came off in her hands, sending her into an ungraceful backward roll. She jumped to her feet and located the snake again. While still holding the snake's rattle, she plunged toward the briars, determined to get a better hold on it. That was when the solidness of Reginald's arm came between her and the briar patch.

"I think it's time to go, Jane."

She had never heard him sound quite like that. She took one anxious glance back at the disappearing snake.

"It can't strike me when it's in all those briars," she explained, but his hand firmly took hold of hers, and she had no choice but to follow him. They didn't speak on the way back, and no mention was made of the rattlesnake, but once they were in his car he proved his mind had been active in other directions.

"Sorry to cut our day short. I must get back to the office and check some things. This stacks up as quite a puzzle—a genuine puzzle." His tone and face had become more serious.

"Can I help?"

He turned a penetrating glance on her—so piercing she grew flustered.

"I could use help. I need to go over everything and find out where this is coming from. If someone wants to sully my name or my publishing reputation, he'd bloody well better get his act together because I'm on to him now."

His sudden passion startled her, and she again saw the formidable side of Reginald.

"Jane, I'd rather not tell anyone else, not even Anna, until I know what's going on. If you want to come by the office for a while, I could definitely use your help."

"I have the rest of the day free. Cody gets back tonight, and we'll go out then, but I'll leave a message for him to pick me up at your office. He lives in Panama City, anyway, and it'll save him a trip. Drop me at my house. I'll change clothes and meet you at your office shortly."

"Are you certain you want to get involved in this matter?"

"I *am* involved. You're my publisher. You can't do me any good in jail. Besides, José saw me too. If he realized the bag on my belt contained a snake, it wouldn't be difficult to learn my identity. There aren't that many snake collectors who roam these woods. That coachwhip acted rather lively, and José kept looking at the bag."

"I noticed that, and it worried me. I'm still worried."

Chapter 4

*Never write checks to companies with
crooked letters on their van.*

Jane made a frenzied search of her closet for the right getup to take her through the afternoon and evening ahead. Reginald's reaction, not Cody's, loomed uppermost in her mind. Considering all of the humiliation she had suffered at Reginald's hands, she could now regain some of her dignity. Cody didn't notice clothes anyway.

Feverishly she discarded one choice after another. She would have to wear something simple so that Reginald wouldn't think she had overdressed or tried to impress him. It also had to look dramatic enough to undo those times he had seen her with dirt on her face and snake on her hands. She had almost concluded that she owned no such dress, when she came upon a thin, white knit. White, exactly what she needed to feel clean and tidy—the very things she had never been when around Reginald. He had blatantly sprayed a scented air freshener into his car after she and her snake had vacated it—as if the coachwhip had left its scent behind. The man infuriated her.

A quick shower and a dash of perfume brought her self-esteem up monumentally. She had enjoyed the day in spite of everything. It was fun to have things happen—anything. The work on her book had helped satisfy that craving, and now this new incident had captured her interest and concern. Although she classified Reginald as a walking catastrophe, an irritating, insulting, argumentative, walking catastrophe, she would never consider him boring.

She slipped into the white dress—a color she would never choose for a long evening with Cody. He wasn't a dress-up kind of person. Oh well, it looked nice and Cody would no doubt love it. Maybe it would produce a new spark in a relationship that had troubled her almost since the day she had accepted his ring.

By the time she reached Faircloth Publishing, she had deep twinges of self-consciousness. They grew decidedly worse when she pulled the office door halfway open and heard a familiar voice call out, "Let me know when my redneck arrives, Anna. I have some matters to go over with her."

Startled, Jane froze in mid-step. Had Reginald meant her? Her ego fell with a thudding crash. She wanted to close the door and make a second entrance or no entrance at all, but it was too late.

"May I help you?" Anna greeted courteously. All at once, recognition dawned on her face. "Oh, Miss Pate, I believe Mr. Faircloth is waiting for you. He's in his office." Red spots appeared on Anna's pleasant, ample cheeks.

Jane plunged into his office, determined to put the ordeal behind her as quickly as possible.

"Jane . . . *Jane?*"

His eyes emitted a singular flash of wonder, and then amusement filled them to overflowing. Her swift, defiant glance warned him it was no time for wise cracks.

"Let's go out for coffee, Jane, and talk about those new ideas. Had any lunch?"

"Not yet."

"Any of those peanut butter sandwiches in your purse?"

"Not today."

"Well, I'll treat this time."

Within minutes, they entered a dark, cozy restaurant. After the outside glare of sunlight, she could hardly see where to walk and appreciated his guiding hand as they weaved their way to a small, secluded table.

"I chose this restaurant because of its privacy, Jane. I need to talk with you about this José matter. I may have put you at risk."

"Have you learned anything?"

"I discovered that I wrote a five hundred dollar check to a

Lubin Cruz less than a week ago. Most likely I gave it to this Webb bloke who pretended to be Lubin. He definitely wasn't Hispanic. Of course, *Webb* is probably a fictitious name too. I have to learn the identity of this man and uncover what kind of a blooming scheme he perpetrated."

"Do you think you should get police help?"

She kept her voice low and wished Reginald would do the same. His words seemed to carry all over the room.

"If I went to them *now*, it could get in the paper. They could even charge me with a crime and lock me up. There could be other evidence against me—things I don't have a hint about. Someone is framing me, Jane. It would have worked perfectly if we hadn't gone out there. For that matter, it may *still* work perfectly."

"You must have some idea who it is, don't you?"

"It could be some old offense of mine that's returned to haunt me, but I doubt it. I'm guessing it's something to do with my publishing company. I told you I often print books that tread on people's toes. I publish books to better people's lives in some way, however small. That's my first and only goal in publishing. Sometimes my writers get involved in rather touchy subjects. Sometimes I make people angry. Sometimes there's big money involved."

"You think these happenings are related to a book you've published?"

"More likely a book in the works. People don't usually go to this much trouble for revenge. If I had a book coming out that threatened someone's reputation or financial security, one of those factors could cause this. It would depend on the seriousness of the threat. I almost convinced myself that someone used my name as protection in case the marijuana was discovered, but the check convinces me otherwise. It already came through my account, and the bank made a copy of it for me. What do you think?"

He held it out for Jane's inspection.

"You've written *supplies* on it," she almost whispered as she squinted to see it in the dark surroundings. "What did you buy from this Lubin or Webb or whoever?"

"Left-over office supplies from a liquidating furniture store— or that's what I supposed. You see, last week a man called my office and said he represented Factory Interiors. I knew the place. It's a couple of blocks from here. Their windows have been papered over with liquidation signs for at least two months. The man said they had a few items left that had to go before they could complete the liquidation process. He offered them to me for almost nothing, my place being the closest business that would use those types of supplies. He had boxes of file folders, envelopes, paper, and an excellent office copier, almost brand new, that would have cost well over a thousand dollars. The paper items alone were worth at least six hundred. Of course I took everything off his hands for the five hundred dollars he requested."

"Did you go into the store?"

"No, he said he'd already locked up. He met me at a white van parked in front of it. It said Factory Interiors on the side of the van, and all the supplies were in it. I asked him if he wanted to sell the van too, but he declined."

"You're such a careful man."

"Publishing is gambling, Jane."

"Did he deliver the supplies?"

"He helped me load everything into my vehicle. Look, he gave me his card." Reginald dug it out of his wallet. "See, I was careful enough to get his card."

"Oh yes, I like that card design too. I bought some sheets of them the other day for business cards."

"It isn't a regular printed card?"

"Here, look at mine. I believe his printer prints slightly higher quality than mine does. Don't you think the green border sets everything off nicely? He must have liked it too. At least he has taste."

"Promise me one thing, Jane."

"What?"

"If I'm jailed, don't visit me."

"They also have stick-on letters in the same department stores that sell these business card blanks. Could the name on the van have been stick on letters, maybe *black* stick on letters, black being the most common type?"

"Black letters, yes. I remember noticing that one word sat slightly crooked. But you see that all the time. Who would pay it any mind?" He shook his head and looked thoughtful for a second. "Yes, they were probably stick-on letters, and no, I didn't look at the license plate—beat you to that one. But it was a white Ford van, a cargo van, and fairly new."

"What about the check?"

"This Webb bloke obviously gave it to Lubin to buy marijuana seedlings, though five hundred dollars wouldn't buy much, not seedlings, not even seeds. They evidently wanted my name on a check for evidence and just used a token amount to accomplish that. Lubin must have taken the check straight to my bank and cashed it. He, of course, had a driver's license for identification—if the bank bothered to ask for it. The situation looks bad. When they catch Lubin, he'll tell them about me. I think I have this figured correctly. The question is—when will Webb double-cross my marijuana farmers?"

"Ssh, Reginald, there could be a police officer at the next table. You still have the supplies and the copier you bought. They're evidence on your behalf."

"The printer looks brand new, Jane. No one would believe I bought it and all that other merchandise for five hundred."

"Maybe it *is* brand new. Maybe we could locate where it was purchased. That's a substantial purchase. Someone might remember something. Let's go see." Excitedly, she rose from the table.

"Jane, we haven't eaten. We haven't given our order yet."

"I think they've lost us here in the dark. We could come back when they're not so busy."

"Okay, let's go."

"You have your cell phone. You could call some places first. Of course this Webb could have gotten it from a second-hand place or from some other city."

It took several calls, but they located an office supply place on the other side of town that carried the same equipment. When they arrived at the store, they found the manager staffing the sales counter.

"Sold one last week," he confirmed when Reginald questioned him about the printer.

"Can you tell me anything about the purchaser? Did he pay with a check or cash? Would anyone remember anything about him?" Reginald asked impatiently.

"Just a minute, let me check." He went into a back office and after a few minutes returned with a sales slip. "He made a cash purchase."

"No name then," Reginald moaned, his clenched fist rested on the counter as if he intended to do someone harm.

"We always have a name," the man said nervously. "We require names on large purchases for warranty purposes. His name is Reginald Faircloth. I believe he's some kind of publisher or something like that—Faircloth Publishing."

"What did he look like?"

"I hardly remember the man. An ordinary looking guy—dressed well."

"Yes. That's him. Thank you for your help."

Reginald turned away with a hopeless expression, and Jane could barely suppress her laughter in spite of the seriousness of the situation.

"Well, Reginald, at least you have a warranty."

Reginald turned back abruptly and approached the man again. "*I'm* Reginald Faircloth. Do you remember selling me the printer?"

"Well, yes, now that you remind me. I guess I forgot what you looked like. So many people come in here."

"They'll throw away the blooming keys," he said to Jane as they left for the second time.

"Look at it this way, Reginald. You bought a new, thirteen hundred-dollar printer and all those supplies for only five hundred dollars."

"This is big. I have to think big, Jane. I believe I need a private investigator."

"That would be wise. Now what books are due to come out? You'd better check those first."

"I have maybe thirty books in different stages of readiness—another fifteen newly assigned, like yours. It'll take a long night's work to go through all of those."

"You can probably eliminate quite a few immediately—mine for instance. I could look at those pending books for you, or whatever helped most."

"I don't think you should involve yourself in this matter

anymore, Jane."

"I'm glad to help until Cody gets here—that'll be seven o'clock. If you plan to hire a private investigator, you need to organize yourself. You need to have a few leads ready for him to check. Working at your office for a while won't involve me any more than I am already. Is there a room there where I could work inconspicuously?"

"Very well, I accept your help graciously because I don't want anyone else to know about this, and because I'd never make it through all that material without aid. You can start on the books. Make a list of any you consider troublemakers. Later, while you entertain Cootie . . ."

"*Cody*."

"Yes, while you entertain *him*, I'll look at any you haven't studied. Right now, I'll go through my files, my finances, my personal papers, phone messages, everything. We must keep this matter quiet from everyone, understood?"

"Definitely."

"Are you ready to dine now?"

"Die?"

"Dine—eat."

"I'm not very hungry. I'd as soon get to work. Cody will take me to dinner, and if I eat now, I'll spoil my appetite."

"You're sure?"

"Positive. Let's get started."

Jane poured over manuscripts in a small back room used primarily for mailing packages. At five o'clock when Anna and the other employees left for the day, Reginald moved her to the conference room where he worked.

"I'm making notes as I go," Jane mentioned a couple of hours later, breaking the silence. "When Cody comes for me, I'll leave my notebook, and you can see what you think. I've found two, so far, that could be troublesome, but I still have all of these to look over."

Jane anxiously glanced at the clock. It was already seven-thirty and no sign of Cody. She wanted to be the first to hear when he arrived so she could rush out and leave no opportunity for introductions. If he lingered, Reginald would talk with him, and Reginald might say anything. Minutes later two headlight beams finally did turn into the parking lot. Reginald was on his feet and out the front door before she could get around the table.

"That must be the Cootie chap. I'll bring him in," he called back to Jane. "I say there, Cootie, come right in. Jane's here. I'm Reginald Faircloth—Jane's publisher."

"Hey, thanks. Good to stretch my legs. That drive sure gets tiresome."

Jane threw her purse strap over her shoulder and rushed toward the door, but Reginald had been too quick for her. He steered Cody into the office and pulled the door closed behind him.

"Ah, here comes Jane, looking for her welcome kiss. I guess two weeks feels like forever to you two."

Reginald stood there with a smug look on his face, his arms folded in front of him, and watched both of them.

Jane felt herself sinking into the carpet. Both men looked at her. Cody looked as if he expected her to make the first move, and Reginald . . . just looked. Finally Cody stepped forward, and she prepared herself for whatever amorous effort he might attempt.

"Say, do you have a restroom in here? Guess I should have stopped at that last rest stop, but I didn't want to get out in the rain."

"It's down this hall. Follow me and I'll show you," she said, relieved and chagrined at the same time.

It was hardly what she had expected from Cody, but at least she had escaped Reginald's eyes for a minute. After she showed Cody the men's restroom, she sequestered herself in the woman's restroom across the hall. One quick glance in the mirror showed her how red her cheeks had become. She repeatedly threw cold water in her face to erase any signs of embarrassment and waited for Cody to exit the restroom.

Finally she heard Cody leave, but she stayed for a few more minutes to give Cody and Reginald plenty of time to get on another subject. With Reginald bent on making Cody's acquaintance, she had little hope of getting away early. Cody, being his usual neighborly self, would sit there all night and talk with Reginald if he got a chance. She knew Cody all too well.

When she returned, she could tell that Cody liked him. She could also tell that Reginald meant to prolong Cody's stay at the office.

"How about some coffee, Cootie? You've had a long drive. About five hours, wasn't it?" Reginald asked as she attempted to navigate Cody out the door for the second time.

"More like six from where we work."

"Oh, you must have gotten off at one-thirty. That's jolly. Gives you a splendid long weekend."

Reginald had not hesitated with his one-thirty. It was as if he had a calculator in his head or had figured it out beforehand.

"Well, not exactly one-thirty. Bad weather cancelled our work today, but I was late getting to bed last night, so I slept in this morning and left at twelve-thirty today. Lost an hour this evenin' when I stopped to eat."

"Jane hasn't eaten. Probably starved by now. She . . ."

"We'd better get going, Cootie—C-Cody. Mr. Faircloth has tons of work to finish."

"That's quite all right, Jane. I have plenty of time."

"Say Reg, we're having a barbecue at my parent's place Sunday afternoon. We've invited everyone. Come on by if you have a chance. Here, take this card. It has their address and phone number. Call if you get lost."

"Thank you, Cootie. Sounds like a good time. I'll try."

"We're going over to the bowling alley now. If you get through here, come on over. You and I'll have a game."

"Splendid idea, Cootie, but I probably won't make that. You'd better take Jane for some din . . ."

"Goodnight, Mr. Faircloth." She grabbed Cody's arm and steered him to the car before Reginald could finish his sentence.

"Nice, friendly sort of guy," Cody said as they started on their way. "Got a strange way of talking, though."

Cody was easy going, a guy's guy. Often she shared his company with one or more of his buddies. She knew he would rather bowl with Reginald than with her. Actually, *she* would rather not bowl at all. It wasn't what she had in mind for the evening, but at least he was home for a couple of days.

"Bill and Marcia will meet us at the alley—that is, Marcia will be there if they can find a babysitter. You can get something to eat over there. Can you bowl in that dress? It's sort of short and tight.

Looks good though. You look real good." He reached his arm around her and kissed her on the cheek when they stopped at a light. "I've missed you. Wish I had a job closer to home." When he saw the light was still red, he put his arms around her and kissed her on the lips. "This every other weekend stuff gets tiresome."

"Maybe I could drive over there on the in-between weekends. It's not far."

"I wouldn't want you driving there alone. New Orleans has some pretty rough spots."

"There must be safe places outside the city where I could get a room for a night or two."

"I don't know. It's a long drive."

Noting his disinterest, she dropped the subject.

"We'll be married soon. Maybe I can get more home time then. Or maybe we'll get a place over there." He patted her shoulder.

She didn't answer. A move to Louisiana would ruin her plans of writing more Florida books. She wanted to write a whole series of books after she finished her reptile and amphibian book—books on birds, mammals, fish, and other such nature guides. Of course, she would have to convince Reginald that he should publish such a collection.

At the bowling alley, she settled for a hotdog, took her turn at the lanes, and soon realized her thoughts had ventured far from the evening ahead. The recent happenings with Reginald both excited and worried her. It could be a threatening situation. He had treated it more lightly than it actually was. He didn't seem to take himself too seriously. Contrary to that, he apparently took his business reputation very seriously, indeed.

When Bill and Marcia arrived, Jane tried to focus her attention on her present surroundings. Marcia plopped down beside her to put on bowling shoes.

"Boy, it's great to get away for a while. We would have been here sooner, but for the sitter."

"Will I see you and Bill at the barbecue Sunday?"

"Yes, we'll all be there, the kids too. Hope it don't rain. Do you plan to carouse with Bill and Cody when we leave here tonight? Bill knows I can't go because our sitter can't stay that late."

"No one's told me anything about the evening plans." Jane felt piqued that Cody hadn't mentioned anything to her. "Carouse where?"

"Bill just said they were going out on the town after we left here. I assumed he meant you too."

Jane grew more pensive as the bowling continued. Conversation lagged, and it was still early in the evening when Cody abruptly put down his ball and changed out of his bowling shoes.

"Time to quit this place," he announced. "Jane has a long drive home."

"Oh, did you drive to town, Jane?" Marcia asked.

"Yes. I was working at my publisher's office."

"Marcia, why don't you drop Jane at her truck on your way home," Bill suggested. "I'll ride with Cody. We may stop somewhere, but I won't be home too late."

"Yea, you're going off partying without us." Marcia said.

Cody embraced Jane and kissed her goodbye. "I'll pick you up at noon Sunday for the barbecue. Expect to see a heap of people there. They've invited everyone in the county."

Jane felt hurt. Not only had he cut their evening short, he didn't plan to do anything with her on Saturday. She had especially wanted to spend time with him—to free herself from recent misgivings.

"Would you rather I just *met* you at your parents on Sunday. It would save you driving all that distance twice?"

He missed the sarcasm in her voice and jumped at the suggestion.

"Sure, good idea. I need to help them set things up, anyway. See you then." He kissed her again, and she left with Marcia.

"They could have at least invited us fishing with them tomorrow," Marcia said sulkily. "I've become a fisherman's widow lately."

"Cody never said anything about fishing."

"You'd better keep tabs on that man of yours. They grow much worse after marriage."

Jane laughed but didn't feel like laughing. Everyone liked handsome, fun Cody. What troubled her tonight? Two months ago, when she and Cody made their decision, marriage sounded wonderful. Now they were already growing apart. No, she corrected, *she* was growing away from Cody. Cody hadn't changed. He wouldn't notice any change in their relationship.

When Marcia dropped her off at her truck, Reginald's car was still there. A faint light shone through the small front window of the publishing house. She felt genuinely sorry for his trouble. Maybe she could help some more on his investigation. She definitely didn't feel like driving home yet, and memory of a distant hotdog suddenly gave her hunger pains.

Chapter 5

It is easier to meet a deadline if you are alive.

Goaded by a strange impetuosity, she drove to a nearby restaurant and ordered a pizza, two salads, and some hot breadsticks. Fifteen minutes later, when Reginald responded to her timid knock at the office door, she realized her instincts had guided her aright. Framed by the dim office light, He looked tired and haggard. His tie was off, his hair rumpled, and his sleeves and collar unbuttoned.

"Cootie gave out early, huh?" He ushered her through the doorway with ill-disguised haste. His manner, not his speech, conveyed the menace of his situation afresh. He studied the outside world for an instant before he locked the door behind them.

"He had a hard day. He was beat," she lied.

"Oh, indeed. Hadn't seen his girl in two weeks. Slept late this morning after a late night out with the boys. Drove six grueling hours in an air-conditioned car—probably has cruise control. And now he has to toddle off for more beauty sleep?"

"He had things he needed to do," she lied again.

"Where'd you dine? I say, they must have served skimpy portions if you're already popping out for pizza."

She didn't answer that time. She forced a weak smile and turned away.

"I'm sorry, Jane. I need to have a wee chat with Cootie."

"*Cody*," she corrected, irritated he had somehow guessed her state. "I hope you like this kind of food." She spread her offerings on the conference table and managed to control her give-away eyes.

"Well, *by Jove*, Jane." He looked up for a brief second, his face dared her to question his word choice. She stared off innocently, and he smiled satisfied. "By Jove, you've made me feel like a heel. I've failed you worse than Cootie. I took you into a place and never let you eat."

"I'm the one who insisted we leave, so I'm at fault. Now I'm here to see if you need more help. I have the rest of the night free. Even if you intend to go home now, I can keep on here. I'm not sleepy, and I can't get this puzzle off my mind."

"I'm making a night of it. I'm convinced I don't have time to waste in this matter. This banquet was exceedingly thoughtful of you, Jane. I won't forget it. And I *do* need your help. It's depressingly lonely in here." He started on the food as if famished.

"Have you found anything?" Jane asked as they ate.

"I wish I hadn't."

"That bad?"

"Worse than *that bad*. I went over your notes while you were gone. They prompted me to examine more carefully the unfinished book on toxic waste that you marked. In some of the newly completed chapters, the author exposed companies guilty of unsafe practices, possibly even criminal infractions. He used well-documented proofs, named names, and even presented a nice collection of pictures. It's conceivable that one of the places he mentioned in that section could lead us to our Mr. Webb. I believe I'm headed in the right direction."

"That *was* the most controversial of the books I reviewed. The author definitely laid things on the line. He convinced *me.*"

"He had reason to be convincing. About five years ago he lost his only child to cancer, and he felt that toxic waste disposal near his home caused it. His name is Victor Torne. I believe I mentioned him to you. He's the one who died in the house fire about a week and a half ago."

"How did that happen?" She gave him her full attention.

"His house burned one afternoon while his wife, Mirta, was at work. They found his remains in his bed and attributed the fire to cigarette smoking in bed."

Reginald's tone had implied much more than the context of

his statement.

"And Mirta?" Jane couldn't stop her imagination. "What did she say about that?" A chill scurried up her back.

"She confirmed that he smoked, but never in bed. She said he sometimes wrote all night and often napped during the day—on the sofa. The fire evidently burned fast and furiously. She lost him and everything."

"How complete is his book? It seemed almost finished."

"Eighty percent. I planned to finish it myself. He put together a solid piece of work, and the widow needs the money. He intended to write two more chapters, but I could complete it with just a summary chapter. Regretfully, all his notes and research burned in the fire."

"How about pictures?"

"I should have most or all of those. He brought me his newest ones, plus his newest chapter, the morning of the day he died."

"Well, speculating that his tragedy *wasn't* an accident and was related to his book, I don't see how it could have anything to do with the marijuana. If the perpetrators wanted to destroy evidence, couldn't they just as easily break in and rob this place—or burn you out too? That would complete the job. It shouldn't be necessary to frame you."

"In this case, such destruction wouldn't sufficiently remove the evidence. I keep discs of all pending projects, including discs of all photos, in a safety deposit box. I have always followed that safety practice. Writers can be notoriously careless. I know of one who would have lost all his research and two years of work if he hadn't just sent his publisher most of his material."

"Were you that publisher?"

"No—the writer. I hate to think what would have happened if the publisher had lost my work."

"But a stranger wouldn't know about this security measure of yours. How would someone know you have Victor's material in a safety deposit box?"

"That very question convinced me that this affair must be related to his book. While you were gone, I went through last month's office calls. Anna keeps records of everything. I found one from the

Torne's attorney, dated the day after the accident. He'd requested information about Victor's book—where we stored it and when we would publish it. Since I'd just looked at your notes on that book, the message captured my interest. I dialed Anna at home and asked her about that call and a few others that could prove important. She remembered it. Said she let him know that everything was in a safety deposit box, even Victor's newest photos and writing, and that I would complete the book for Mirta.

"I called Mirta a couple of hours ago and asked her if she or her attorney could have mentioned to someone, to anyone, that Victor's work was in a safety deposit box. She couldn't remember imparting that information anywhere. She went on to say that her attorney definitely couldn't have told anyone because she doesn't *have* an attorney."

"Oh boy." She stopped eating and stared at the table full of papers. "I hoped we'd find some simple reason for all of these happenings."

"Like *what*, Jane?"

"Like maybe you have a split personality, and one half of you is a compulsive marijuana dealer. Or like you stole someone's girlfriend and fell victim to revenge. Or maybe you . . ."

"Cootie doesn't have it in him," he interrupted with his worst know-it-all manner.

"*Cody* doesn't have any reason to worry on that score. He trusts me." She punctuated her proclamation with a large bite of pizza.

"Cootie's a dolt. *I* wouldn't trust you if *I* were Cootie. Not even with that five-and-dime ring on your finger. Women never know what they want."

He sat back with a self-satisfied air, his arms folded across his chest again. His eyes invited her to jump into an argument. She had only meant to put some levity into the conversation, but it had calamitously turned toward the personal. Temper control presented her greatest challenge with this man.

"You're stepping on toes again," she warned as calmly as possible. "You do that often, don't you?"

"Constantly. It gets me into some blithering messes."

"Like this marijuana trouble? It's hard to believe any of this could be true."

"Not so hard. I've been there before." He stared at the wall behind her with an unfathomable expression on his face.

"Not *this* bad, I hope."

When he reached for the last piece of pizza and hummed, Jane groaned.

"That scar on your leg, is *that* a souvenir from one of those blithering messes?"

"The result of a bullet wound." After putting his pizza slice down, He unbuttoned his shirt and exposed a brawny shoulder with another jagged scar. "This one caused me considerably more concern, but it missed the heart anyway. Are you sure you want to work around someone like me?"

"Are they b-both from the s-same incident?"

"Same plight." He looked up at her and began buttoning his shirt. "Pardon me, Jane. I didn't realize that my undressing would embarrass you."

"You didn't undress. You showed me a scar on your shoulder."

"You blushed."

"I don't blush, and it—it's galling of you to say I did. Do you always blurt everything out like that?" She wished there was pizza left so she could throw it at him.

"When it's true. I'm an exceedingly poor liar. Actually, you're not very good at it either."

"If this is *truth* time, tell me about Zaire." His smug answers and her curiosity about him finally outweighed her discomfiture.

"Zaire? Let me see now. Zaire is actually the Democratic Republic of the Congo. Its national products are coffee, palm oil, rubber, diamonds, gold, and silver. The life expectancy rate there is . . ."

"*Reginald!* I know about Zaire. What were *you* doing there?"

"A rather lengthy piece on the poaching situation. You should know a *little* about that—that is, if you stayed in school long enough."

His eyes danced, inviting a fray again. She gritted her teeth to keep back the sharp retorts that begged to be set free on this man.

"Even we unenlightened snake catchers have heard about the

white rhino, the mountain gorilla, and the elephant—how they're wiping them out in record time. It's quite a problem there. Did you stay long?"

"I hadn't intended to. I researched extensively before I arranged the trip and just wanted some good pictures and a modest amount of local flavor." He thumbed nervously through the papers in front of him and a subtle change came over his voice. "Things became slightly more involved. Anna's husband, John, taxied me around in a small aircraft. That's where he was shot, killed." He drew a deep breath as if it had been hard to get the words out. "The trip was supposed to take a month. It took two years for me and an eternity for John."

"Was John killed by poachers?" she asked sympathetically, but still determined to hear the entire story.

"Our third day there."

"But you stayed two years?"

"I had work to finish. I realized I had only half of a story and hadn't covered the best half yet. I stayed and continued my research. Regrettably, in my hunger for more knowledge, I took a seat at the wrong banquet table with no formal invitation. I explained to my hosts that it was a mistake, but they decided I should remain with them anyway. That was the longest dinner engagement I ever endured. When I finally decided that dessert wouldn't be to my liking, I bade my hosts a fond farewell. They regretted my departure so much they insisted I take these gifts along to remember them by—or perhaps to speed me on my journey." He signified the wounds on his leg and shoulder.

Jane's mind swam as she tried to read between the lines of this strange recitation. It felt like a game of charades.

"They captured you? Shot you? The poachers?"

"The rebel forces, over the diamonds."

"What diamonds?"

"The diamonds they sell on the black market all over the world."

"I thought you were doing a piece on poaching."

"So did I, but it became all mixed up over there—corruption, uprisings, poaching, diamonds, money laundering, drugs—a mammoth muddle."

"How much of those two years did you spend as a guest of a rebel army?"

"About nine months. It was in the news and in my book."

"Book?"

"Jane, some writers consider it good policy to learn something about a prospective publisher and publishing company before submitting proposals. You know, to see if they're right for said publisher and said publisher is right for them."

"Reginald, I *knew* you were the right publisher the instant I heard about you."

"Yes?" His face brightened with surprise and expectation.

"Definitely. I had already submitted to all the others and had been rejected." She smiled shamelessly and turned quickly to her papers.

Reginald threw up his arms in despair. Immediately his huge laugh shook the office.

"You know, Jane, you can carry this honesty thing too far." He laughed on and applied a handkerchief to his eyes.

"Shall I study Victor's book now and see what names and places I can find?" she asked demurely. Her curiosity temporarily satisfied regarding this man, she was almost *afraid* to learn any more about him. "Do you have Victor's newest pictures or are they all in the safety deposit box?"

"I have duplicates of them here. I'll get them for you." He smiled. "I appreciate you're being here, Jane. I hope you realize the risk *now*."

He hesitated as if he had more to say but instead procured the material she requested and returned to his own tasks. Jane labored painstakingly as the hours rolled by. By six o'clock in the morning, she had finished the book and had made a list of all businesses mentioned, plus detailed notes about each one.

"I've marked the ones that seem most likely, including all the ones that have been photographed," she said and handed Reginald her findings.

He studied the list carefully. "I'll investigate these. If it's chemical offense were looking for, we need to know how much offense. I need to know how much damage this book can do. Could something in it cause financial ruin for someone? A pile of health lawsuits? Maybe a prison term?"

"Obviously something like that—considering the measures taken to prevent its publication. I didn't find anything in any of the pictures, but I don't actually know what to look for. There are white cargo vans visible in three of the photos, but many businesses use white cargo vans. That's probably no help."

"I'll make calls today and probably do some heavy driving on Sunday to visit some of these plants while they're closed."

"Reginald, what would happen if they arrested you for dealing in marijuana?"

"On an operation as sizable as this and in this state? Law enforcement would confiscate everything I own—and me."

"What would happen to your pending books?"

"They'd most certainly be delayed. Probably never come out. The writers could eventually peddle their material elsewhere, but it's not easy to secure a publisher. Most of the books would drop by the wayside, and Victor's would be one of those. There'd be no one to finish it. Mirta isn't qualified, nor would she care to attempt it."

He looked down at his desk and pondered his next words thoroughly.

"To convict me of an offense like this is the perfect way to keep one of my books from being published. It would work more effectively than killing me, though that could be part of the plan too since I might prove my innocence. Then again, I don't know what other evidence has been put together. Maybe I couldn't prove anything."

"There has to be more than one person behind this, considering all that's transpired."

"Yes, and definitely big money and big risk, involved. Look at what happened to Torne. I'm convinced that neither the fire nor Victor's death happened accidentally."

"They've moved fast, haven't they?"

"In a week and a half's time they've eliminated Victor and his book, investigated my real estate holdings, located my acreage, and planted a large marijuana crop. They've also set me up to pay a marijuana dealer—with a *check* no less. They now know I keep copies of all Victor's material in a safety deposit box, they know what I look like, and they've even obtained *pictures* of me—all in a week and a half. Yes, I would say they've moved fast." He brought his fist down on the table.

"And José will swear you checked on your crops. They obviously plan to notify the authorities about the marijuana, but how soon?"

"Soon, I think."

"We'd better consider what else they could possibly do to frame you."

"Precisely. I mustn't waste a minute. Even if I could get out from under such charges, it would cast a doubt about me, probably ruin my reputation, maybe ruin my business. They may know about you too—if José talked. Jane, you shouldn't be involved anymore. The situation could get rough."

"If you go under, so does my book."

"A book's not worth your life. I don't want to lose any more writers. Go home, Jane. Get some sleep and forget all of this. What will Cootie think if he finds you spent all night with me in the office?"

"Why should it matter? I'm innocent of any wrongdoing?"

"I didn't plant that marijuana either."

"All right, I'm leaving."

While she found her purse, he waited at the office door and took her hand when she reached for the doorknob. His eyes flashed with a softened light.

"I have a better idea. Let's get some breakfast. The pizza was fantastic, but now it's only a fantastic memory." He drew her near and kissed her forehead. "I'm sorry. I'm not ungrateful—only scared for you."

He held her close against him briefly. She stared at the nothingness of his office wall from over his shoulder and chastised herself for being moved as much as she was.

He locked the office behind them, took her arm, and steered her to his car. She nestled wearily back against the soft leather seat and couldn't stop the thought that it should be Cody there beside her, watching a new day lighten. She leaned her head back and sighed.

She could feel Reginald's probing eyes. Why didn't he drive off? His hand came over hers and gave it a gentle squeeze. It felt warm against her cool one. When a hard little ring made its presence known, he smiled briefly and drove out of the lot.

They found a breakfast bar open, and both rushed to satisfy their hunger with little ceremony.

"I see you're not a diet-drink-and-salad girl." He laughed at her loaded plate.

"For some reason, I'm ravenously hungry. I hope it's okay to go back for more."

"We'll go together."

A second plateful satisfied her hunger, but he made it through three with no trouble. The amount of food he put away amazed her, yet he wasn't in the least stout, just sturdy, incredibly sturdy. She was glad he dove into his food with such abandon because it took his attention away from her. Ordinarily she would feel nervous about her table manners when eating with a man who wore Armani and drove a Continental. His *redneck* designation still echoed in her ears.

When they finally left the pleasant atmosphere of the restaurant and drove back to the office and her parked truck, she could feel Reginald's serious mood return.

"Jane, I'm worried about you. Why don't you lie low for a while? Go visit someone. Go back to New Orleans with Cody. No—bad idea. I need you where I can keep an eye on you."

"Listen. *Don't* worry. I have work to do. I have a deadline to meet with my publisher."

"I had a writer cross over a *dead line*. That makes it serious, Jane. I especially don't want you to traipse alone in the fields. What if someone followed you?"

"I'll use care, whatever I do." She opened his car door and stepped out.

"Is that the best promise I can get from you?" He leaned toward the open door. "Look, I intend to check places in central and north Florida Sunday. Would you like to come along? I don't want you involved, but I'd feel better if I knew where you were."

"I'm to attend a barbecue with Cody on Sunday, remember?"

She regretted the barbecue obligation. It would be much more interesting to help with the investigation. She closed the car door, but he immediately rolled down the window on that side.

"Give me your cell phone number so I can reach you

anytime."

"I don't have a cell phone right now."

He immediately dug into his glove compartment and brought out a small cell phone and charger. "It's an extra. Promise you'll keep it with you everywhere. I'll make sure you can reach me at all times."

"Will you let me know if you learn anything?"

"Of course."

The look on his face seemed to give a completely different message from his spoken words. She began to suspect he would try to limit her involvement and her knowledge of anything he discovered.

"Do you plan to look into the meeting José told us about? At the shack?"

"It's not safe, and I'm having doubts about your safety. You shouldn't go home alone. Why don't you get back in and let me drive you there. You can pack a suitcase, and I'll get you a room in town. I won't be able to sleep if I know you're out there alone."

"I've things to take care of at home, and I *do* have neighbors."

"So did Victor, and we can't be sure José hasn't talked—though I don't think he did. He's a smart boy, and I somehow trust him. I hate to think he may go to jail."

"I know. I feel the same. I have to go now."

"Wait a minute, Jane. If I gave you more expense money, would that persuade you to stay in town?"

"Probably not, but I'm not adverse to extra pay."

"No deal. But I've meant to talk with you about venomous snakes. You could be bit when you're out there alone. You take enormous risk. I've witnessed that, and now you have a new threat. If I paid more, would you stay in? Or take someone with you?"

"Good bye, Reginald."

She jumped into her truck and pulled into the lane of traffic. Almost instantly she remembered her still unsigned check. "I need that money," she said ruefully and looked back just as he pulled away from the parking lot and disappeared around a corner.

Jean James • Mary James

Chapter 6

Never spy with a bagged rattler.

Reginald's intrusive attitude left Jane more than perturbed. He had actually tried to curb her snake collecting. She knew her work held certain risks, but many jobs incurred the same, and she used care. When she stopped at Marcia's house fifteen minutes later, her feelings still chafed from Reginald's lack of support.

"Hey, Jane, you missed Cody. They left about an hour ago. Cody slept here since they got in so late last night."

Marcia sorted apparel in her laundry-and-everything-else room while her two toddlers squabbled with each other amidst the piles of soiled clothes.

"I had a crazy, hectic week at work. It left me too tired in the evenings to do anything, so I let my laundry go all week. Now I must pay the price."

"Can I help?"

"Oh no, I'm complaining because there's someone here to listen—a luxury I seldom have. What will you take to the barbecue tomorrow? I can't decide whether to cook something or just buy chips. Bill and Cody hope to catch fish for it. Maybe I'll be lazy and let them take care of it."

"I think that's a good idea. After all, you're here working, and they're out playing."

"I don't mind. I don't really like to fish anyway. I'm glad to have time at home to do the things *I* want to do. Don't you feel that way when you're not working?"

"Not really. I love my work. I'd rather work all the time."

"I can't understand *that*. Snakes—ugh. Give me laundry any day. When you finish this book, that will be it, won't it? Cody said you'd probably do something more civilized."

"I hope not. I have ideas for more books if I can persuade my publisher to go along with them. Hopefully I can still tramp around the countryside."

"What will you do when you have children?"

"I'll take them with me—and walk slower." She laughed. "I'll find a way to handle it. I don't plan to stop my work."

"I don't know about that. I have trouble holding onto these two just going to the grocery. Maybe you should look for something tamer. Say, Jane, why don't you stay overnight tonight? We can all party here when the guy's get back."

"I have too much to do today, Marcia. I don't think I can, but thanks anyway. I've got to go now."

Marcia doesn't realize how much her words irritate me, Jane thought as she hid her hurt feelings. It was bad enough when her parents pestered her about collecting. Now her publisher and her closest friend had added their disapproval, both on the same morning. She felt too tired to trust herself not to get into an argument. After a brief goodbye, she drove home to her bed.

Late in the day, she awoke to the ring of the borrowed cell phone. She sat groggily up in her bed to take the call.

"Look out your window," came Reginald's familiar accent through the receiver.

"Why?" she asked sleepily and pushed damp curls back from her face. The fan spewed hot air across her bed on that scorching afternoon. Even her pillow was drenched.

"Do it, Jane."

She walked to her window and saw the long, brown car in her drive. Reginald leaned casually against a front fender, his phone to his ear. He saw her at the window and waved. She ducked out of sight in panic. One wet, dilapidated curl hung over her eye to warn her how her hair must look, and she wore her oldest shorts and a ripped blouse. When she glanced in her mirror to learn the worst, a friendly beam of sunlight shone through the bedroom window and burnished the golden-brown curls that crowned her drowsy head.

There's no time to change, and he's seen me worse, she thought. *My face looks clean anyway.*

She stepped barefoot onto the warm grass and sauntered lazily across the yard, blinking at the last remnant of afternoon sun. She met two penetrating eyes, alive with unspoken compliments.

"My house is clean. Would you like to come in?" she suggested, frustrated by his scrutiny.

"Not a social call, Jane. I'm here with an ultimatum."

"Well, ultimate away. You have my attention."

"I'm not sure. You look half asleep."

"Half of me is better than no me at all," she said dreamily.

"I never settle for half, Jane. See this nice cool car here?"

"How can I help but see it. It fills my whole drive. If my landlord sees it, he'll probably raise my rent."

"He may see it because it will be parked here all night with me in it unless you come with me now and let me take you to someplace safe. Just for a few days, until I get this puzzle worked out. I can't embark on anything if I'm worrying about you out here alone."

His voice carried a more serious tone than usual.

"I'm not your responsibility, Reg."

"I'll tell Cody about the entire situation, and let *him* talk sense to you. Why isn't he here now?"

"Because I didn't invite him," she lied and smiled a crisp, neat little smile. "I needed to get some rest."

"Don't talk drivel. If you were *my* fiancée, I'd be here, invitation or not. Where did you find this joker? I may not know the man that well, but I did meet him, and I like to think my observation skills are reasonably well developed. I'll wager you didn't meet him at church. Remember, Jane, it's difficult to walk side by side with someone unless they're on the same path."

She turned her back to him and started to walk away when his hands caught her shoulders. It was like the shock of ice water down her neck, and she couldn't stop the shiver that rippled through her body. He didn't release her, and she could feel him close behind. In a minute her eyes would betray her with the hot tears that struggled to escape. He folded his arms in front of her, gripped her forearms tightly, and brought her close to him.

"I'm sorry that I'm messing up your life," he said gently, and she felt his lips against her hair.

She took a deep breath to gain control of her emotions.

"I have a safe place I can go tonight."

Her voice sounded husky and strange to her, and when he took his arms away, she felt as if he had ripped her in two. She stood there, coldly stoical, and worked fiercely to hide her feelings.

"Can I give him a thrashing for you?" he asked, and turned her toward him to look deeply into her eyes.

She blinked in bewilderment. He must have thought her agitation came from disappointment in Cody. He must never know what she had felt—and she must never let herself feel like that again. She couldn't make herself smile. She felt sad and resigned, deflated like a life raft that had torn itself against sharp rocks.

"Thank you for driving all this distance to check on me," she forced out listlessly, again in full control of herself.

He looked at her questioningly, but her camouflage was up. She had turned her face into an impenetrable mask, as dull as the sky above that had just lost its last glimmer of sunlight.

"I'll pack now. Remember you promised to call if you learned anything?"

"I'll call whether I learn anything or not."

"You don't have to wait here for me. I'll get ready and leave right away."

"I'll leave when you do," he said stubbornly and sat down in his car.

Immensely irritated, she hurriedly packed. She would have to go to Marcia's. She didn't want to see Cody, especially since Cody hadn't asked for her and didn't expect her. To put her in a worse mood, Reginald followed behind like an armed escort. "Delivering me to the arms of Cody," she said as she drove along and wondered why she felt so drained and unhappy. Reginald stayed with her until she pulled into Marcia's drive. Only after she had stepped out of her car did he drive off. She ignored his wave.

Marcia greeted her gladly, and together they prepared some

dishes for the next day. When they finished that, Jane helped her clean her house. Whenever conversation wandered toward Cody or reptile collecting, Jane quickly changed the subject.

"You're awfully quiet Jane. Don't you feel well?"

"I worked most of the night, and I'm awfully tired."

"Why don't you take a nap?'

"Sounds good, but it looks like our fishermen are back."

Together they walked outside to meet the men. Cody, laughing and joking, seemed genuinely happy to see her there. She soon detected a strong smell of alcohol and realized the giddiness wasn't just from joy at her presence.

"Look at this catch, will you. Now it won't matter how many show up tomorrow."

She spent the next two hours helping Cody clean fish while Marcia and Bill went to the store for snacks and movies. Cody talked constantly about his day and never noticed she responded in monosyllables. She doubted he would notice if she didn't answer at all. After a while she only half heard what he said. She was diving deep into her own thoughts, trying to understand herself. She didn't mind cleaning fish, she *liked* cleaning fish, but at that moment she would rather do it by herself. Restless and tired, she wondered how she could endure the long evening ahead. She made up her mind to excuse herself as early as possible and go to bed.

That evening they sat through two new releases—movies that, in her opinion, never should've been set free on the movie going public. The first one started out boring and cheesy, but soon became morally offensive. She dozed through most of the second one. When she and Marcia finally turned in, Cody and Bill started in on computer games.

She didn't know what time they finally went to bed, but everyone was asleep when she crept out the next morning and left a note saying she would meet them later at his parent's house. Too unsettled to be around Cody, she drove miles into the country to think and to find some illusive answers. She had shoved aside dozens of considerations for too long. The time had come to deal with her doubts. Marriage couldn't be treated lightly. She felt angry with herself for waiting until someone had to remind her who she was.

Hours later, she arrived at the party, still unsure of many things but at least in a better mood. She had made peace with herself and hoped that she could make a rational decision when the time came. There was no reason for haste. She tried to enjoy the day and spent most of her time with Cody's mother. She had grown fond of the woman.

"Everyone's enjoying the barbecue, don't you think, Jane?" Cody's mother asked for the third time.

"You've certainly outdone yourself. Can I get you more fish or anything?"

"Heavens no. I could pop. Let's sit here and let it settle. I been thinking, Jane, that when you and Cody tie the knot, you need to talk him into getting a job closer to home."

Cody came over and joined them.

"What you women gossiping about over here?"

"I told Jane to talk you into getting work closer to home after you're married."

"I'm hoping *she* works closer to home after we're hitched—instead of traipsing all over creation."

"She's having her fling before she settles down, Cody. Jane's waiting for you to get her a nice place somewhere around here where we can see each other more often."

"I don't know, Mama. Jane's house ain't bad. I've been thinking we could probably arrange to buy it. I could get to the Interstate a lot quicker if we lived there. That would cut some times off my drive to New Orleans. I don't reckon I could make the same kind of money around here that I make there with the oil work."

"Oh, nonsense. There are plenty of good jobs to be had here. Panama City's growing. You could both find work here. Jane, you talk to my oldest daughter, Theresa. She could probably get you on at her company. They pay real good. She says the benefits almost beat the pay. She's had two children since she's been there. The company insurance paid for everything."

In an effort to be agreeable, Jane finally plastered a fake smile on her face and nodded to the conversation going on around her. Everything was falling apart and no one could see it. The day became an ordeal that she wished would end.

Her thoughts strayed to the marijuana fields and the meeting that would take place that night. She wanted to find out who perpetrated this terrible ruse. Reginald had called her an hour ago to ascertain she had attended the barbecue. He sounded discouraged and said he probably wouldn't be back until late. He agreed not to call again *if* she promised to stay away from her house that night. She promised, but didn't tell him where she intended to stay. She planned to sneak back to his river property and see what she could learn about the situation.

After all, she was better qualified for that task than anyone was. She could move around in the woods more adeptly than Reginald could. Whenever she chanced upon people of unknown character in the woods, she simply melted into the foliage until they passed or until she could creep away. Only last week two men passed within ten feet of her and never discovered her presence. Most intruders meant no harm, but she always felt safer not risking discovery. She knew that she, more than anyone else, had the experience needed to spy on this Mr. Webb.

The picnic felt interminable. She must make some definite plans. It annoyed her to sit there and have her serious work treated like an indulgence or a fling—as Cody's mother had called it. She couldn't blame them, they were all nice people and meant well, but she felt hurt and trapped.

When she and Cody first met, she had still been looking for a publisher. He hadn't minded the work she did, and he always acted happy-go-lucky about everything. He would go along with whatever she wanted to do as long as it didn't interfere with what *he* wanted to do. Now he seemed slightly different. Maybe their approaching wedding date had caused it. Maybe she was different too.

"I don't think she heard a word you said, Cody. She's a million miles away."

"Oh, I'm sorry. I'm just tired. Did someone say something to me?"

"We want you to persuade Cody to stay longer. He plans to leave our party and head back to Louisiana."

"Jane, I should start back now. I need some sleep before work tomorrow morning."

"That's all right Cody. I'm beat myself and don't feel well, but I hated to leave early on your last day at home. I believe I'll go now too."

"Uh-oh, now we've lost both of them. Guess we fed them too well. They've gone lethargic on us."

She and Cody said their good-byes, and the thought kept going through Jane's mind that it hadn't always been like this, not back when they first started dating. Three months ago he would never have left. He always stayed the limit, stayed until he could barely make it in time for work on Monday morning. Now, this weekend, they hardly saw each other, and it didn't bother him. It didn't bother *her* much either, but she blamed that on her extreme concern over Reginald's situation.

Once out of sight of the gathering, she grew wide-awake and thrilled to get away so early. Since she always kept collecting gear and clothes in the back of her truck, she could drive straight to Reginald's land. It was only three o'clock, so that left plenty of time to look things over and decide if she possessed nerve enough to spy on the meeting that night. She wondered how late the meeting would take place. *Night* could mean anytime between six in the evening and dawn tomorrow morning.

When she arrived at the second parcel of acreage, she parked across the road from it in the same secluded spot they had used the last time. She carefully drove her truck far back into the trees and faced it outward in case a quick exit became necessary.

After changing to her collecting clothes, she stuffed only the most necessary items into her pockets and belt—reptile bags, flashlight, knife, and cord. She wanted nothing that might hamper her progress if she had to hide or run. She drank from her water bottle and left it behind, but decided to take the rake. If it hindered her progress, she could always drop it.

Before searching for a hiding place, she wanted to look over both parcels of land and make sure no one else was around. Following the stream branch all the way to the river, she searched for boats. The river appeared deserted, but many trees hung over the water, and a boat could easily be moored out of sight or even pulled ashore. She crept along the bank all the way to the shed and stopped there to study the surrounding woods painstakingly before she ventured further.

Carefully circling the marijuana patch, she ascertained that no one worked in that field. She hurried to the other parcel of land and to the patch where they had met José. The place looked deserted, but she saw evidence of recent work. Someone had set out another large field of plants. The new field almost adjoined the field where José had worked. When totally satisfied that no one else was there, she worked her way back toward the shed, following the edge of the swamp and collecting as she went.

The area had an abundance of blue-tailed and broad-headed skinks. She experienced more luck than usual catching those fleet reptiles and attributed it to the seclusion of the area. Evidently, no human predators had ever disturbed or hunted these reptiles. Maybe no one had ever walked through that lush, ferny spot, so tranquil and dreamy in the afternoon sun. Only a few birdcalls and the hum of insects disturbed the silence.

All at once her heart jolted in her chest. An exceptionally large diamondback rattlesnake lay stretched out, asleep, on a high bank at the edge of the swamp. It blended so well with its surroundings, she had almost passed by without seeing it. She studied it carefully and estimated it to be just over six and a half feet long. In all of her collecting, she had found only one other diamondback of that size, and this one was still unaware of her presence.

Tremulous, as she always felt upon a special find, she snatched the largest bag from her belt. Softly she crept to a nearby bush and secured the top of the bag to its spiny branches. It took less than a minute to adjust it to her satisfaction with its top open and the bottom resting on the ground. The snake now showed movement in its head and tongue. It had felt the vibration of her steps in spite of her caution. Wide-awake now, it sensed danger.

She quickly took the cord from her pocket and tied it to one of the middle prongs on the rake. Holding the other end of the cord with her left hand, she brought the prongs near the snake's head. It struck the rake once and reminded her of the danger she entailed. She hastily maneuvered the cord around the snake's head and drew it tight until she had pinned the snake's neck against the metal end of the rake.

Keeping pressure on the cord so the snake couldn't free its head from the rake, she lifted it above the bag. It was almost too long and heavy to handle at the end of a rake. It whipped its thick body around violently and knocked one side of the bag loose just as she thought success was at hand. She quickly lowered the snake to the ground, maintaining tension on the cord as best she could, and reached with her left hand to attach the bag more securely.

In spite of her efforts, the snake managed to free itself. This time it moved fast and started to disappear through the underbrush. She raked it back into an open area near the bag. Thoroughly aggressive with rattles vibrating fiercely, it coiled and struck twice. As it poised its head to strike a third time, she managed again to loop the cord around it. The cord closed perfectly against the snake's neck, and she raised it into the air above the bag for the second time. When she had managed to lower most of its body into the bag, the weight and wiriness of the snake prevailed again. Bag and snake toppled to the ground, and the rattler darted its head out, bent on fight or escape. She released the cord and pushed the rake towards the snake, causing it to draw its head into the bag where the rest of its body remained enclosed. Instantly she blocked the opening of the bag with the rake, prodded the snake to withdraw further into the bag, and knotted the top.

"Whew! Luckily no one saw that, especially Reginald or Cody." She looked at the bag as if she expected the snake to reply. She couldn't contain her delight that she had safely, or somewhat safely, collected the snake. At least she had kept risk to a minimum. It would have been easier to pin its head to the ground with the rake and just pick it up, but that always involved more danger, especially on a snake as large and strong as this one. The experienced professional who milked them for the antivenom laboratory had lost that gamble six times, but then he had a ready supply of antivenom. Since she was usually far from help or antivenom, she intended to continue using her sloppier, safer method.

At least she had never let any venomous snakes escape, that is, except for the one Reginald made her leave behind. She had slightly lost her head with that one. Somehow, it had become a twenty-dollar bill that was getting away, not a snake at all. She laughed silently at the memory of it—and this snake would bring close to thirty dollars. Yes, there was always risk, but the elation superseded it and goaded her to go back repeatedly. Inevitably, caution evaporated in the thrill of the chase.

She slid the bag's knot between the prongs of the rake and carried the rake over her shoulder as she continued collecting. The area yielded two water snakes and a mud snake of unique design. Instead of the usual red belly and rows of red markings that travel part way up each side, this one had markings that traveled entirely around its body in brilliant red bands. She also found many toads along the edge of the swamp, so she left the toad bag unknotted and constantly added to it as she worked her way back.

The day proved so successful, she almost forgot the job at hand, but sight of the shed brought all her caution back. She scouted the area carefully and checked the river again for boats. No fresh marks gave evidence that anyone had pulled a boat ashore, and no fresh footprints showed in the dirt surrounding the shed. If a meeting was set for that night, it hadn't taken place yet.

Safe for the moment, she searched for a good hiding place, a retreat that would enable her to see and hear everything, but not close enough to get her into trouble. The swamp didn't offer much cover. The heaviest foliage in that vicinity grew directly against the back and ends of the building itself. In fact, the growth clung so tightly against it that it would be difficult to squeeze in. She deliberated a minute and wondered if she should dare. The best place to hide appeared to be the worst for escape.

With her body pressed against the building, she worked her way along until she reached a spot that allowed more freedom of movement. Inevitably, it was located directly at the middle of the long back wall, and she could see nothing.

She had no way of knowing whether the meeting would take place inside the shed or outside. They might inspect the marijuana field before they talked money. If she intended to use her present location for a hiding place, she would have to clear a passage for a noiseless exit in case they didn't come into the shed at all. She also needed a peephole so she could watch anything that might transpire inside the building.

Though she could find no visible holes on the wall, the old plywood had many rotted areas. In a convenient spot about eye height, she used her knife blade to whittle a small opening in it. When she pressed her eye against it, it gave her an adequate view of the room. The hole also lined up with the doorway on the other side of the shed and afforded her another opportunity for viewing, provided they came before dark. If they came after dark, she guessed they would use a light. Somehow, she must see this man's face, *all* their faces, if possible.

It took a few minutes to clear a slightly larger area for standing and to make a narrow pathway to serve as her lone escape route. She hid the bagged diamondback and the rake in the densest foliage at the side of the passageway where they wouldn't be seen and where she wouldn't accidentally step on them. The rest of her bags, she kept on her belt.

Satisfied with her preparations, she ventured forth to watch the river. Along the muddy bank, she added to her toad collection until there were at least thirty toads in the bag. At a nickel each, they didn't add up to much money, but it gave her something to do. She also needed a few to feed the hognose snake—*Reginald's* hognose snake. She smiled at the thought.

About an hour into darkness, she began to think no one would come. Probably José had told them about Reginald and her, and they had changed their plans. Maybe they even now watched to see if anyone would come to spy on them. She must use extreme caution because they might come from the road this time and not use a boat at all.

She studied the darkness in the direction of the marijuana, searching for pinpoints of light. They would have to use flashlights if they came now. Webb would probably want to make sure they had planted the marijuana. She wondered how long he would wait before he reported the crop and implicated Reginald. Or would he wait at all? Maybe this meeting marked the final step before he set the wheels in motion.

Weariness began to tell on her, and she wondered if she might wait all night for nothing—well, not *totally* for nothing, since she had made some excellent collections. Maybe Reginald had learned something on his trip that day. She hoped he hadn't tried to call again because the cell phone rested safely in her truck. It would only have gotten in her way and might accidentally have revealed her presence at the wrong time. She hadn't familiarized herself with it enough to trust it.

The long awaited sound of a boat motor interrupted her thoughts. A hurried glance down the river affirmed that a boat approached. Pushing through the dew-wet branches of her narrow hiding place, she pressed hard against the wall. Her heart had barely stopped its heavy slugging when she heard voices and saw a light flash here and there around the area. *Checking to make sure they are alone*, she thought. The voices became louder and a small beam of light shone through her peephole.

With her eye to the hole, she saw a light hanging from the roof beams, a bright light. Evidently, they saw no need for caution since the shed's one doorway angled away from the river.

Two men brought in bags of fertilizer and stacked them on the floor. They both spoke Spanish, and she realized they must be the two other planters whom José had mentioned. She couldn't find José and wondered if he waited at the boat. She heard one man call the other Tomás, so she could now at least identity José's brother—a nice-looking, young man, probably in his early twenties if that old. The other man, most likely Lubin, looked about fifty.

José must have kept his secret. The two men sat on the fertilizer bags and talked constantly, but she couldn't make out a word they said. So much for the course of Spanish she had taken in school. She could conjugate a verb but that didn't prove helpful in this situation. She surmised that they waited for someone, and that the meeting would actually take place that night. Until that moment, she hadn't really believed it would happen. Now it would unfold, probably right before her eyes, right under the light of that swinging lantern where moths passed back and forth making eerie shadows.

With an effort, she tried to bend her legs to relieve their cramping. She had tensely locked them when she put her eye to the hole and now paid for it. Mosquitoes hummed round her ears, attacked her hands and face, while a few managed to penetrate the back of her double shirts. Even with the loud chorus of insects and frogs, she didn't dare risk slapping at them, so she squirmed and waited and felt thoroughly miserable when the sound of another boat drew her attention. It took Lubin and Tomás longer to notice it, but when they did, they rushed out of the shed and talked more excitedly. She distinctly heard one of them say the name *Webb*. She waited breathlessly, and within minutes, a new man entered the building along with Lubin, no doubt the mysterious Mr. Webb.

"We are ready. If you have our money, we will buy the last seedlings. Everything will be planted by Thursday night, maybe Wednesday," Lubin explained in excellent English and only a slight accent.

"Show me what you've done."

The man who conversed with Lubin was medium height with a slightly stocky build, big chest, and long, heavy arms. His mustache might be false. It looked false. The glasses could be false too. She tried to picture his face without facial hair and glasses, tried to place each individual feature in her memory. He had no jewelry or distinguishing marks. Their conversation proved unenlightening, but they at least talked in English. She mentally kicked herself for not having brought a camera. Probably that cell phone had a camera if she had just bothered to investigate it.

Tomás hadn't come back in and evidently kept guard at the boats. Lubin and Webb walked outside, but she could still hear their voices distinctly.

"We put in two patches on the other land. The one here runs along the edge of the swamp, long and narrow. When we pick up those seedlings, we will plant another patch here, beside it."

"Show me this one. I'll take your word on the others."

After they had left, Jane relaxed slightly but dared not sit or change her position. The chorus of night sounds had abruptly stopped and any slight movement might be heard in the night's stillness. An eternity later she heard them return.

"Better get this fertilizer out of here. Some boater could pull ashore before you have a chance to use it. They might wander in and see the shed. People are curious. Better leave it in the bushes somewhere—cover it with brush. It's not supposed to rain for a few days."

"I'll get Tomás," he said, obviously not wanting to do the task without help.

Lubin and Tomás carried the fertilizer around the building to the very brush where she hid. Webb held the flashlight and barked commands.

"Throw it back in there and toss some branches on it." He waved his flashlight toward another pile of debris. "There. Get that old door over there and drop that on it. Make it look natural."

Tomás pried the door from the dirt while Lubin pulled dead branches from the tree that hid her from their view. She held her breath. The flashlight beam might expose her at any second. When Lubin reached for another branch, a dead limb fell so near Jane's bag it alarmed the rattlesnake. Its warning rattle penetrated the night's silence.

The men froze for an instant and so did Jane. Almost instantly she heard exclamations in Spanish and English.

"Tomás, get a shovel from the boat," Lubin hollered as he turned his own light into the brush also.

Jane watched aghast as the beam invaded the privacy of her hiding place, touched the snake bag, and finally came to rest on the rake lying close by her feet. She looked for an escape route, but they stood in front of the only one.

"Look!" Lubin called when the light found Jane.

Jean James • Mary James

Chapter 7

*If you collect toads after midnight,
beware the snake in the grass.*

She plowed straight into the brush in the opposite direction, hoping the impetus of her body would make the briars and branches yield. She stumbled, caught her feet in vines, but continued to fight her way toward freedom.

Lubin reached her before she could get clear of the thicket. Wiry and agile, he grabbed her, pinned her arms behind her, and shoved her toward the shed. Excruciating pain shot through her upper arms and shoulders when she tried to break his grip.

Webb followed them in and snatched the bags from her belt. "What's *she* doing here? What's she got in these?"

The open bag of toads spewed all over the floor. When he took one of the other bags and started to unknot it, the snake in it whipped around, searching for a way to escape.

"Augh!" he shouted and dropped it to the floor. "A snake! It's another snake!"

With a shaken, angry gesture, Webb turned and approached her. In desperation she used all the force of her right leg to kick him in the face with her heavy boot. Lubin jerked her away while Webb fell to a seat on the floor. He looked fiercely up at her, swiped a hand across his bloody mouth, and spit out what looked like a piece of tooth. Jane watched fascinated as the piece hit the floor and one of the toads immediately lapped it up, thinking it an insect."

"What will we do with her?" Lubin asked.

Webb didn't answer but rose slowly and came toward her. Rage distorted his face hideously.

"See how you enjoy a little *boot*."

He kicked an enormous foot at her face. Her reflexes on edge, she saw it come and jerked head and body violently to the side with all the strength in her. The big boot connected with Lubin's neck and sent him sprawling and gasping in pain while Jane dove for the open door and straight ahead into the swamp. She knew the area, knew she was at an advantage even without a light. Their encounter with her rattlesnake would unnerve them somewhat, and they wouldn't plunge into a swamp as freely as she would. She ran fast and as silently as her surroundings would allow. The crashing noises behind her sounded close, much too close for her to chance hiding submerged in the knee-deep water where their flashlights might find her again.

Suddenly a loud cracking sound and a splash to her left drowned out the sounds of pursuit behind her. She saw their light beams turn in that direction but couldn't see any cause of the noise. When she realized they thought the sound came from her and that she had gone that way, she swerved to the right. Now she headed straight toward her truck and couldn't hear sounds of anyone following her. Voices rang through the night, but they sounded distant. They had certainly gone the other way.

Not ready to trade caution for speed, she constantly stumbled and fell over unseen objects. Soon the ground grew swampier, and she struggled through water and ooze that reached halfway up her thighs. When the water level reached her waist, she grew disoriented. She stopped and silently listened for sounds of her pursuers. The loud slap of a beaver's tail sent a shock wave through her, but pinpointed her location—she had waded into the beaver's lake.

She changed direction again, struggled out of the swampy area, and made a beeline across the remaining woods. Branches and thorny vines slapped and ripped at her face and clothes, but still she ran. With her key out and ready when she reached her truck, it took only seconds to vacate her parking spot and fly down the road without the aid of headlights.

Terror over of what she may have caused rather than over

her narrow escape enveloped her so totally she couldn't think. Her blunder may have precipitated Reginald's undoing. Maybe now he wouldn't have time to find the proofs he needed before Webb put his vile plan into action.

Could she ever put this terrible night behind her? She had learned nothing, had been caught spying, and had lost her rattlesnake and other catches too—though they didn't matter much anymore in the sum of things. She must tell Reginald what she had done—that was what mattered now. Hot tears of anger fell silently on her muddy jeans, and she smeared a hand across her face to clear her eyes

Only when she neared the outskirts of Panama City, did she feel safe about turning on her headlights. With trembling hands, she dialed Reginald and instantly heard his anxious, "Yes?"

"Reginald, I . . ." Her voice quavered in spite of her efforts of control. She took a breath and forced herself to calmness. "Can I see you tonight? It's important."

"Jane! Where are you?" His words pounced at her.

"Not far from your office."

"Don't go there. Go to my home. There's someone there to let you in."

He gave her his address, but no friendly *goodbye* followed, just the silence of an ended call. He had sounded edgy, almost brusque, and she wondered at his shortness, wondered if she had irritated him by calling him at night and demanding to see him. Probably his investigations hadn't gone well that day, and now she would load more trouble on him.

"You'll be much angrier when you hear my story," she told the sleeping phone.

His house stood just off the highway, a giant, two-story affair with substantial columns at the front—an utterly intimidating dwelling. She pulled hesitantly into the long circle drive and stopped at the massive front door. When she walked into the beam of the entrance light, she looked down at herself. Only then did she notice the head-to-foot mud, the rips in her clothes, and the pieces of forest still adhering to her. She ran her fingers through her hair and felt dried chunks of mud. Reluctantly she pressed the doorbell.

The door opened on a scene of comfort far exceeding that of

Reginald's office, complete with ultra-plush carpet, subdued lighting, and an attractive woman lounging on the sofa with a magazine. Said woman had an air of artificiality about her, like the mannequins in exclusive department stores whose half-human eyes followed you reprovingly, saying that *they* knew you couldn't afford to shop there even if nobody else in the store did.

In due course, the bona fide, flesh-and-blood woman who had opened the door brought Jane's attention away from the ethereal scene. Sixty and plump, with her face showing a bit of shock, she found her voice.

"Hello. . . . May I help you?" "Mr. Faircloth asked me to come here," she divulged, uncomfortable with the situation.

"Won't you come in, please?"

"I c-can't. I've had an . . . an accident, and I'm all . . . could you just tell him I'm here?"

"Marie, let me take care of this," came a voice from the sofa, which proved it wasn't a mirage or mannequin but an actual, live woman who sat there. She rose elegantly and made her way to the door. "Whom did you wish to see?" She stared haughtily at Jane.

"Mr. Faircloth." She somehow couldn't call him Reginald in the face of this awesome mansion and this disdainful woman. "I just called him. He told me to come here."

"Reggie hasn't called about anyone coming . . . has he Marie?" Without waiting for an answer, she continued, "Reggie's not here. No one's called all evening."

"I called him on his cell phone . . . about fifteen minutes ago. If he's not home, he must be on his way. I'll wait for him out here. I'm rather a mess."

The woman made no comment, but her eyes said she agreed. Her straight, regal body continued to bar the entrance as if she were Gabriel, and Lucifer had asked admittance to paradise. Only after Jane reached her truck and looked back, did the suspicious stare change to a smug one and the imposing door close with finality.

Humiliated, Jane sat on her front seat and waited. She decided the *mannequin* woman must belong to Reginald since possession was written all over her. She couldn't blame the woman for uncordiality in the face of such a disreputable appearing caller.

The woman probably considered herself Reginald's protector, his defense against some weirdo, and she had called him *Reggie*. *That* must be why Reginald didn't want her to call him Reggie. It was *this* woman's pet name for him.

Jane waited and felt more miserable by the minute. Wretchedness had thoroughly set in by the time Reginald arrived thirty minutes later. He never shut off his motor but jumped out and headed straight for his front door.

Jane bit her lip and opened her truck door. He must have heard because he did a quick about-face and rushed to her.

"Jane. I thought you were waiting inside."

The obvious concern in his voice left her almost speechless.

"I . . . waited here. I'm too mussy to go in."

It was then she noticed he was in his safari suit, as she had been calling it, and looked almost as untidy as she did.

"Get in my car, Jane."

He took her arm and led her to it. She could sense the restrained fury in this man, and it frightened her. When he opened the door for her, she shook her head.

"I can't. I'm covered with mud."

"So am I. Get in."

The sternness of his voice intensified her vulnerability. She stumbled onto the immaculate leather seat and sat there like a trapped animal while he entered the other side. He didn't say anything but instantly drove away. At a drive-through, he ordered burgers, fries, and drinks. The silence remained while they both ate hungrily.

"Are *your* boots full of mud too?" he finally asked. The slight hint of amusement in his voice and his eyes unbalanced her nerves worse than his sternness.

"Y-yes . . . yes," she laughed and cried at the same time. "Reginald, I've m-made a mess of things. They'll move faster now."

"How did they find you? Where were you hidden?"

"What do you mean?"

"I was *there* . . . in the swamp, hiding, but too far away to see anything very well. I couldn't believe my eyes when I saw them drag someone into the building. When the thought came to me that it could be you, I moved in closer and . . ." he gave her his most disapproving look, "confirmed it. I saw someone kick at you, and somehow you were free and running. I tried to follow at first, but thought better of it and decided to make enough noise to send them in a different direction. When I reached the highway, I thought I heard a car leave, *yours,* I hoped. I waited there to make sure. I was about ready to go back in when you finally called."

"I'd been there since three o'clock. Cody had to leave early."

"You've hid there since three?"

"Not all the time. I checked both places to be sure no one had arrived early or was working the crop. I collected for a while, and later I found a good place to hide against the back of the shed and made a peephole."

"It jolly well couldn't have been that good. They found you."

Anger and exasperation had returned to his voice.

"Not because of my hiding place. I chose a good spot, but they knocked a dead branch on my rattlesnake bag and the snake started to . . . make noise."

"You brought a blooming rattlesnake with you?"

"I didn't bring it. I found . . . it sort of showed up—a big one, worth almost thirty dollars." The expression on his face told her at once that she shouldn't have mentioned its dollar value. "They would never have found me in the thick brush where I hid if it hadn't been for the . . . the s-sound . . ."

"It's called *rattle*, Jane. A rattlesnake rattles. I believe that's why they call them rattlesnakes."

"If it hadn't been for the *rattle*, they wouldn't have turned their flashlights toward my hiding place and seen me. They stood in front of my only exit, and when I tried to make a new path, Lubin caught me before I could get clear." She took a noisy slurp from her drink. "I kicked your Mr. Webb in the mouth."

"Bully for you. I missed that part. I guess what I saw was Webb returning the favor, right?"

"I ducked just in time, and poor Lubin got it instead."

"I guessed that was how it played out. They walked quite near to me when they checked the field, but I couldn't make out their faces in the darkness. I did get a glimpse of Webb when he walked into the lighted shed. I believe he's the same man who sold me the office supplies."

"I got an exceptionally good look at him, and his mustache needed adjustment after I kicked his face. I tried to memorize his looks, all of him. I believe I could identify him with or without glasses and mustache. In addition to his general appearance, he has enormous feet, he's cruel, and he's terrified of snakes. He started to open one of my snake bags. You should have seen his face when he realized what it contained. Oh, I almost forgot. He has a broken tooth, or a missing cap. It's an upper, front tooth. He spit it out after I kicked him. If the snake hadn't shaken him up, I probably wouldn't have managed the kick or my escape."

Reginald sat silently thoughtful for a minute. When he finally spoke, there was new interest in his voice. "Do you think it would still be there?"

"I hope it's still there. I need the money. The bag was tied, so unless he took it with him, it's still there. There were two other bags with snakes too . . . plus the lizards and . . ."

"Snakes? What snakes?" He looked confused, then disgusted. "I'm talking about the *tooth*, Jane, the *tooth* fragment. Do you think it would still be there? It could prove to be valuable. I know it's a long shot at best, but it could give us his DNA, and it could lead us to a dentist and hence to the man. No one goes around for long with a broken front tooth or missing cap. It would hurt and would look unsightly. Most people would go straight to a dentist. Now if I faxed a description of this man and an x-ray quality photo of the tooth fragment or cap to the right dentist, he could contact us before the man got out of his office. Of course, I'd have to contact a good many dentists. It could help. . . . Anyway, it's all I've got. Jane? Stop laughing. Jane!"

"It's—it's all you *haven't* got, not for DNA and not for a dentist. . . . A *toad* swallowed it."

"A . . . what?"

"It rolled past a toad, and the toad lapped it up. They do that. I remember my school days when the boys would roll BB shot past toads. The toads would lap up every one, and their bellies would get so full they'd literally *thump* when they hopped around.

"You mean my only evidence is in . . . is . . ." He doubled over and laughed until the car rocked.

"Reginald, it didn't happen long ago, and there's only one opening to that shed. The guilty toad could still be in there—or close by. We *might* be able to find it," she suggested hesitatingly.

"Somehow I knew you'd suggest something like that."

"It's an outside chance that we'd locate it—very, very outside. We'd have to gather every toad we could find, and we'd need something like a fluoroscope or x-ray machine to examine them."

"My detective, Harris, could probably arrange that. He has all kinds of contacts."

"We'd need to go soon. You rarely find them in daylight, and tomorrow night there'd be no chance at all."

"I realize that. I doubt it's worth the effort, but I'd like to look the place over again anyway. Tell me what to do, and I'll catch what I can."

"You couldn't. You'll have to take me."

He looked at her and shook his head.

"I'm sorry about tonight. I'm truly sorry. At least let me undo some of it."

"No."

"I'll go by myself then," she said stubbornly.

"Jane . . . Jane, I could keep you from going. I *know* you wouldn't kick *me* in the teeth."

"You'd have to tie me to keep me from going, and I *know* you wouldn't do that," she answered indignantly.

"Of course I would. I say, that's a jolly good idea."

Jane couldn't ascertain whether he was in jest or serious.

"He'll be able to find me now—your Mr. Webb. I've gotten in the way of his plans, and he needs to get rid of me. Let me help. Please?"

"You win for now, but I'll call Harris and see if he can go with us as a safety measure. He needs to see the property anyway, and he can keep watch at the car while we work. We'll keep in contact with him by cell phone. Do we need supplies?"

"We'll need lights, bright lights, either lamps or lanterns, and flashlights. Light attract bugs, and bugs attract toads. I'll need a couple of bags unless mine are still there. He jerked them all out of my belt.

That's how the toads got loose. I'd left the toad bag untied."

"We'll go by my house and get what we need. I have lights there, and you can get some bags from your truck. I'll call Harris to meet us there if he can."

They found everything they needed in Reginald's garage. Jane was thankful she wouldn't have to be introduced to the women in the house, an ordeal she would rather put off until she could at least shower and change clothes. When another car pulled in beside them, Reginald introduced the driver as Harris Bair of Bair Investigations, a middle-aged man with gray hair, gray eyes, gray suit, and soft, gray fedora—an old man's hat trying to look cool on a not-so-old man's head but falling somewhat short of the illusion. His ultra-neat appearance contrasted ludicrously with theirs at that moment.

"Harris, let's ride in my car. You and Jane can pull your vehicles around behind my house."

"Give me a minute to slide into some coveralls. I've decided I can be more useful by going in with you. I'd like to have a look at this situation first hand. If this matter were to become a court case before we have things figured, it could help your cause if someone else was aware of these particulars."

"Or we can all go to jail together," Jane said cheerfully and brought a smile to the detective's serious, well-lined face.

Light shone from a widow in the house as a drape was pulled aside. A woman, *the* woman, peered out for an instant. Reginald and Harris both had their backs to the house and didn't notice her, but it gave Jane an uncomfortable feeling as she started off with the two men. She hurried to take the back seat so that no one would get a wrong impression.

At the property, Reginald pulled into a new spot, across from the first field, and Jane realized that was why she never saw his car earlier that evening. They proceeded cautiously to the shed and found the area deserted. All of her bags were gone, including the bag with the diamondback. Even the rake was gone. Only a few toads still hopped about in the shed, and Jane collected them before they escaped.

Setting up the lights, Reginald and Jane started work while Harris kept watch. Within minutes, toads collected around the lights.

"We should search in a wide circle. Some of them could have already traveled a good distance," Jane advised. "Of course, many won't come out at all."

"What size was the one that swallowed it?"

"About the size of this one." She held up a largish toad. "But it's easier to grab everyone you see. I can sell them. They're worth a . . ."

"Jane!"

She heard Harris laugh, and Reginald muttered something to himself that she couldn't make out.

The remaining hours of the night sped by. Just before dawn Jane checked the bags and found they'd collected fifty-six toads. She had also collected two water snakes. Her flashlight beam had exposed them in the shallow water by the bank of the river. She had quickly bagged them and not mentioned it to Reginald. She needed to recoup some of her losses. He wouldn't understand.

"Jane, there's something here hissing at me," Reginald called out. "It looks ferocious."

"Just another hognose snake searching for its breakfast. I told you they ate toads. I'll get a bag."

"For mercy's sake, Jane, stick to the job at hand. Leave the critters alone. We're after these ugly, warty little creatures, and that's all we want."

"No need to waste money. Your friends stole all of my other reptiles."

"I'll give you the money," he pleaded.

She grabbed the snake and stuffed it into a bag. "See. It didn't waste any time at all."

"Let's get out of here before someone shows up. They could come to work early out here."

On the drive back to the city, Jane tried to consider what consequences her actions may have caused.

"Do you think Lubin and the others will be scared to continue now? Won't they think I'll report them?" she asked.

"I doubt it will matter to this Webb. He may tell them he's gotten rid of you," Harris said, apparently having also thought the situation over. "It shouldn't hurt his plans much if you *did* report them now. He's probably set up most of his frame. But if he learns that you and Reginald know each other, he might just decide to eliminate both of you. That's why I wouldn't recommend going to the police right now. Even if you did convince them about this plot, it might only scare Webb off for a short while. He's not going to go far, and he's much too dangerous to ignore. Murder doesn't seem to trouble him, and that would probably become his new plan. Something extremely important drives the man, and until we find out what that is, you're neither one safe."

"I must be crazy to have let Jane get more involved," Reginald said as they approached the city.

Harris arranged for them to take the toads directly to a doctor who had a laboratory. Enduring the misery of their muddy clothes and wet, mud-filled boots, Jane and Reginald waited expectantly while the man examined each toad. It wasn't long before the last toad was popped back into the bag. No toothy objects had been found.

"Maybe I should go back tonight and collect some more," Jane suggested drearily.

"No Jane." Reginald patted her on the shoulder. "I doubt it would help much to find it anyway. The toad's probably miles away, or something has eaten it."

"You're right. That's a possibility." Jane reached to her belt for the bag with the hognose snake. "Reginald found this fellow beside the shed at daybreak. Their diet is toads."

"Stretch it out here, and we'll find out." The doctor seemed unbothered by the fact it was a snake.

"I see the bone structure of two toads, freshly ingested—probably only hours ago. Let me move them around and see if I can find anything." He pressed on the snake's side, turning it slightly. "Take a look at this—this piece here. That may be it. It's larger than I expected. I'll get it for you—may have to kill the snake."

Reginald winced. "Do we have to watch?"

He took Jane's hand and pulled her into the next room where they compared the appearance of the man who sold Reginald office supplies and the man whom Jane had kicked. After establishing, beyond a doubt, he was the same man, Jane wrote a detailed description for Harris to use.

"It's a cap *and* a bit of tooth," Harris said when he came

into their room and displayed the white piece of porcelain. "There's a fragment of broken tooth in it. It could furnish important DNA evidence in court—if we can find the man who belongs to the tooth. It could even lead us to him now. I'll start work immediately and try to find a dentist with an appointment to replace a broken cap. If you can help me narrow the location to a certain area or areas of the state, it will help a lot."

"We'll try, and here's a description of the man. I could probably identify him and Jane definitely could. She saw him clearly tonight."

"I reckon, if she kicked his tooth out." Harris laughed.

When they got back to Reginald's house, Harris left to take care of other matters, while she and Reginald stayed in his car, still trying to assimilate their newest findings. The house hovering close beside them seemed silent and empty.

"Did you find anything yesterday? Jane asked.

"Nothing. I drove all over North Central Florida checking plants. That's the area where Victor last worked. His last chapters covered that area—his last pictures too, dated the day before he died. It was only shortly after he died that I bought those office supplies—and then we found the marijuana.

"Did Victor bring installments to you regularly?"

"No. It had been a month since he'd dropped anything off. I gave Harris copies of all Victor's pictures and of your list of plants so he can check ownership and things like that."

"Any fresh ideas on how Webb found out about the book? Or about you?"

"Harris and I both believe that Victor made someone uneasy when he gathered information and took pictures down there. The worried party or parties either got hold of his name and address through some interview he'd arranged, or else someone followed him when he returned home. Probably the next day they broke into his house, realized his work could be hurtful to them, and got rid of him that afternoon. He'd left new material at my office that very morning. Of course, he would have had the originals of everything at home. Both the manuscript and the pictures would have been on his computer, along with the name of my publishing house. Someone could have followed him to my office too.

"I interrogated Anna further about her talk with the fake attorney. She said he'd *specifically* asked if I'd gotten the newest stuff Victor had done. She, of course, set his mind at rest and told him Victor had brought in new material and pictures the morning of his demise, and that they were safely put away. I haven't told Anna what she may have set off. It would crush her."

"I guess you can assume the plant lies somewhere in North Central Florida, but that's still a large territory to cover," Jane said.

"Yes, but we only have to cover the places Vic listed. He didn't investigate every plant and factory. He just tried to find enough to prove his point, to make a statement. There weren't many factories pictured either, and he'd listed less than a dozen in that newest chapter. The hardest job will be to notify all the dentists and to locate the right one—*if* Webb even goes to one. Someone will have to check that entire area of the state—and around here too. However, if this Webb walks into a dentist office that we've notified, we could have him in jail before he knows what's happening. I wouldn't mind going to the police with all this mess if I could find Webb. Harris said he'd put one of his people on the dentist job right away. "

"I've made things worse, haven't I?"

"You haven't made things worse. You may have accelerated the outcome. You *have* put yourself in more danger."

"All of this trouble because of that snake, but it could have happened to anyone."

"Anyone, Jane? How many people carry rattlesnakes around with them?"

"I'm sorry, but it was six and a half feet long. Do you realize how seldom you find a rattler over six feet?"

"You're obsessed."

"It was a long day. I had to do something while I waited."

"Knitting would have been nice. What on earth possessed you to go at all?"

"You went—and you lied, too. You told me you weren't going."

"I didn't lie. . . . I *don't* lie. I said it's not *safe*. . . . I didn't say I wouldn't go."

"You implied it. And I didn't say I wouldn't go either. Now

here we sit—two honest people."

"And one will retire from this investigation, immediately."

"I don't know what kind of women you're used to," she pictured the *Reggie* woman in her mind, "but I'm not . . ."

"*Clean* women—I'm used to *clean* women who smell of Chanel—not reptile musk. Women who carry brushes and makeup in their bags, not snakes."

"Well go bother *them* and leave me be. I have work to do—*Reggie*." She turned away from him and climbed out of the car.

"Jane, where will you be? Don't go home. You *can't* go home now. Why don't you stay at my . . ."

She slammed the car door shut before he could finish, but he stepped out of his car and shouted, "house."

She shot him a daggered glance and climbed into her truck, but couldn't help one last retort and called out her window, "I'm *wearing* perfume!"

Chapter 8

Jane! Jane! Wherefore art thou, Jane?

Tired, angry, and dirty, she reached for her phone and called Marcia at work. "I need to borrow your house for a while . . . and your shower. You're washer and dryer too."

"Sure. You know where the key is. By the way, where did you and Cody go yesterday? You didn't elope, did you? We all speculated about it when you both left the barbecue early and at the same time."

Somehow Marcia's words struck her as funny. She guessed her extreme exhaustion was bringing on hysterics.

"No," she said, trying to control her amusement. "I never saw Cody after I left."

"Will you be at my place when I get home from work? I thought we might do something this evening."

"I'll probably only be there an hour or two, but I'll call if I can make it back later."

At Marcia's, Jane immediately availed herself of the shower. She stepped, fully dressed, under the hot water. That was easier than trying to wash the mud off her clothes by hand, and she was too tired to make the effort anyway. Finally she consigned the dripping clothes to the washing machine. While she cleaned her boots, she had stormy thoughts about Reginald. Her anger had fast turned to fury. He had no right to run her life or insult her. And she was angry with herself for letting it bother her. Sure, she had messed things up a little, but she didn't intend to leave it all in his lap now. She guessed she *wasn't* the kind of woman he was used to—and never would be.

After she had tossed her clothes into the dryer, she took a nap on the sofa and awoke promptly when they were dry. The half-hour of sleep had renewed both spunk and resolve. She would do what she had to do, come what might. Donning the same clothes, she pulled on her wet boots, and drove straight to the marijuana fields.

She found José on the second piece of property where he prepared a new place for planting. She circled it twice and found no sign of boats or other human life other than José. A careful search showed that José had no weapons. She felt she could handle a weaponless José—or at least outrun him.

"José," she called quietly and approached cautiously.

José looked startled as he searched for the voice.

"José, I need your help," she ventured as she stepped out of the trees and let him find her.

"You not dead?" He looked scared. "Mr. Webb, he talk Lubin. Say he take care of snake lady. Safe to plant now."

"Mr. Webb's a liar, José. He plans to double-cross all of us."

"You tell Lubin—he come later."

"No, Mr. Faircloth doesn't want anyone to know that I'm his friend—only you, José. He trusts you. What else did Lubin tell you?"

"He say snake lady hide in woods. Maybe see marijuana. Maybe tell police. But Mr. Webb see Lubin this day, early. He say you gone now, not to worry. Lubin think maybe he kill you. We all scared. Wish we no plant here."

"I saw Mr. Webb kick Lubin. Is he ok?"

"He sick—hurt neck bad. They go get more plants. Come back later."

"Did Mr. Webb bring Mr. Faircloth's check?" Jane asked, gambling it *was* a check.

"Sí, same like last time. But no same name."

"You mean that the check had a different signature on it?"

"Lubin say name—Tea-man. Lubin angry. Mr. Webb say he must drive long way to bank. No same bank."

"Do you know where the bank is?"

"No. You ask Mr. Faircloth. He know. Mr. Webb say Mr. Faircloth use other name sometimes, other bank, sometimes. I think Lubin go Alabama."

"José, you must be careful. When do they meet with Webb again?"

"He say *Mr. Faircloth* come next time, bring much money, cash money. Come Friday. We all meet Mr. Faircloth Friday."

"Yes, Friday night at the shed," she gambled again, waiting to see if José corrected her. She didn't want to appear too uninformed. "Also, José, Mr. Faircloth sent you this." She brought out eighty dollars of her own money and placed it in José's hand. "We weren't sure how much we could trust you. Mr. Faircloth thanks you. You can help us catch Mr. Webb in his double-cross."

"Gracias. I like Mr. Faircloth. I help."

Jane could see the high regard José felt for Reginald. She realized this boy had known few heroes in his life, and few benefactors.

"What about Mr. Webb?" she asked curiously. "You have met him, haven't you?"

"Meet Mr. Webb one time—no like. I spy now for Mr. Faircloth."

"Watch close, José. If anyone comes, you run fast. You keep a good lookout while you work. Mr. Faircloth will try to protect you if anything happens."

She thought to herself that even if Reginald didn't, she would. She liked this wise, trusting boy. She hated to see him mixed up in this crime. Her regret caused her to add one last thought.

"José, you'd be a smart fellow to leave right now and go back to regular farming, or something else that you liked."

She had just gotten back into her truck when the cell phone rang. Reginald was calling. She definitely didn't want to talk with him, but fear that he might have a new problem convinced her she should answer.

"Yes," she said reservedly.

"Coldness doesn't become you, Jane. Where are you?"

She wasn't prepared for that question and hesitated.

"Where are you, Jane. Don't lie."

"I'm sitting here resting. I'm in a safe place."

"What safe place?"

She couldn't think of an answer. In frustration she cut him off, started her engine, and drove quickly toward the city. The phone rang again, and she gritted her teeth and tried to ignore it. On the fifth ring she gave in and answered it with silence.

"What safe place, Jane?"

"I'm driving. I'm on my way to a friend's house where I plan to get some sleep."

"Don't you consider me a friend? How about *my* house?"

"I need a less demanding friend right now. I'm tired."

"Come on, Jane. Don't sulk."

"I'm not sulking."

"Come to the office. I'll wait for you."

"I need a nap."

"Do you want to know about the tooth?" When she didn't answer, he asked, "How far are you from the office?"

"I'll be there in thirty minutes."

She looked down at her clothes. If she showed up in her work clothes, he might wonder where she had been, but nothing in her suitcase seemed quite right for this meeting. A nice business dress would boost her confidence. She would have to stop and buy a cheap one since there wasn't time to go home.

"Are you still there, Reginald?"

"Yes, Jane."

"Give me an hour . . . no, an hour and a half, okay?"

"Jane, you don't have to dress up for *me*."

She was sure she heard him laugh. Even after she had turned the phone off, his laugh echoed in her ears. He was—infuriating. She should have left the mud on her clothes. But now, she had to know about the tooth. They must have learned the man's identity."

In less than twenty minutes, she arrived at his office. She made no apologies for her clothes and even grabbed her disreputable hat at the last instant and crammed it on her head. Anna opened the door and smiled warmly.

"Mr. Faircloth is in his office."

He stood in his doorway with amusement in his eyes. She grew angry at sight of him.

"What did you learn?" she asked.

"Let's take a ride," he commanded more than suggested as he picked up a folder and started out the front door.

She followed him to his car, excited to know about the tooth.

He opened the car door for her, and as she seated herself, he lifted her hat and tossed it into the back seat.

"Curls look better," was all he offered in explanation, and she tried to hold her temper until she found out about the tooth.

He never started the car, but sat back and studied her for a minute. "Where have you been this morning," he finally asked.

"Well, I collected toads in the woods until dawn. Next I stopped at a doctor's laboratory to . . ."

"*After* all that. *After* you refused my hospitality."

"I cleaned the mud off."

"Obviously. What then?"

"Have I asked you where you've been?"

"I'll gladly account for every minute if you'll do the same."

"Sorry. I only came here to find out about the tooth."

"I knew that would fetch you, but first let me show you something."

He handed her a colorful sheet describing a five-day, four-night cruise to the Caribbean. She studied it in confusion.

"There's a ticket in this envelope. Your boat leaves tomorrow."

For the first time in her life, she was too angry to speak. She grabbed her hat and reached for the door handle, but he seized her wrists with hands suddenly hard. All of him had become hard.

"I don't want to hurt you, Jane, but by heaven, I'll lock you up in my storage shed if that's the only way to keep you safe."

"Well, *by heaven* beats *by Jove*, but where did you get such colossal nerve?"

"A necessity of survival."

"The publishing game couldn't be that rough."

"Any game can be rough; it depends on how you play it."

"What did you find out about the tooth?"

"Nothing . . . yet."

"What! You said . . ."

"I asked if you wanted to know about the tooth. That's all I said . . . Is that murder in your eyes, Jane? Usually I find it frightfully hard to read your face, you hide your feelings so well, but I believe I've learned to read your eyes." He held her tightly, but he used a softer tone. "Take the cruise, please, and if you want to take your book elsewhere, I'll find you another publisher. Right now I'm not sure how this dashed mess will come out."

"Don't insult me. I have things I need to do. I really don't want to act unladylike and get in a rough-and-tumble with you."

"Could be fun."

Jane laughed in spite of herself.

"You're stopping the circulation in my hands."

"Sorry. But I need some kind of assurance from you that you'll be safe. I can't let you go till you promise me *something*."

"I'm on my way to New Orleans—to see Cody."

She jerked her hands away and opened the car door.

"Stay in New Orleans until I call. I'll let you know if it's safe to come back."

"I'll stay there as long, or as short, as I choose."

She slammed the door, got into her truck, and rolled all the windows shut. After she started her engine, she called him on her phone. He watched her, and when she saw him pick up his phone, she waved at him.

"Reginald."

"Yes, Jane."

"You'd better check through your papers again." She pulled out onto the road and continued to talk as she sped away. "You just wrote another five hundred dollar check, this time using an alias. Your other name is Tea-man, spelling unknown, and your Tea-man account is probably at a bank in Alabama. Mr. Faircloth will meet with his farmers in person this Friday evening at the shed, at which time He will pay them big cash. Mr. Webb got rid of the snake lady and told them to go ahead with their planting. Lubin will cash your check today, and José almost has the ground ready for the new seedlings. José said to tell you 'gracias' for sending another eighty dollars. He will keep watch for you and keep his mouth shut. He *likes* Mr. Faircloth."

She felt good about indulging in that small piece of revenge. The man needed taken down a little.

"Jane, you'd bloody well better get back here."

"Bloody, hard luck, Reginald. Sorry. No time. Much work. Long trip."

"Jane, you've never seen me angry."

"Try a cruise, Reginald. It'll cool you off.

Chapter 9

Never follow an amiable Frenchman to a New Orleans' bar.

At a roadside park, Jane dug into her suitcase for something cool to wear. She joyously traded her sweltering jeans and turtleneck for a pair of yellow shorts and a sleeveless top. After throwing her wet boots in the back of the truck and donning some sandals, she felt ready for the long trip.

Only a short distance into the long monotonous drive, she began fighting to keep awake. The thirty-minute rest at Marcia's had only taken the edge off her tiredness. Now exhaustion hit her full force. She struggled on until near the halfway mark, gave out, and stopped at a rest stop for a nap.

Later she awakened to the sounds of a baby crying in the car beside her and discovered she had slept almost three hours. Heat radiated around her in spite of her open windows and the lateness of the day. She bought a cola and pressed the cold can against her hot cheeks and forehead as she continued on her way.

Some fifty miles later, she began to wonder at a white car behind her. That same car had followed ever since she left the rest stop. Even when she pulled off for gas, it had followed. She knew it wasn't unusual to see the same car for long periods of time on the Interstate, but this one stayed too consistently in the same spot. It made her nervous. Soon it would be dark, and there would be no way to distinguish it from other vehicles. Some autos had already turned on their lights.

Whether she drove fast or slow, the car stayed at the exact same distance. When it turned on its lights, she noticed its left beam shined slightly dimmer than the right one. That would help her keep track of it if it continued to follow after night set in. Apprehensively she pulled into the last rest stop before New Orleans and watched as it followed suit.

She found an empty parking space in front of the building, between two cars, and pulled into it. The white car took a space further down, and no one vacated it. She rested and waited for it to leave or for its occupant to fall asleep. Sleep was out of the question for her. In anger at Reginald, she had turned off her phone, and now she wished for *anyone* to talk with. She turned it on and waited expectantly for a friendly ring, but knew Reginald had probably given up on her long ago.

When total darkness set in, she pulled back onto the Interstate. No car followed, and she breathed a sigh of relief as she studied the headlights in her rear view mirror. Just as she began to relax, a set of lights pulled out of the rest stop. She recognized them instantly.

More than scared now, she wanted to call Reginald, but he was almost six hours away. She couldn't call the police just because the same car followed behind her all evening. With sufficient gas to get to the motel where Cody stayed, she decided everything should be all right if she avoided any stops.

By flashlight, she tried to read the directions to Cody's motel that his mother had given her. His parents were history buffs and had visited him once when they toured Ft. Jackson, which sat far out on the same peninsula.

The traffic grew heavy. Unsure of which lane to use, she remembered that Mrs. Strickland had said it became tricky where you crossed the Mississippi and to be sure and make the correct turns. Her efforts to read the map, watch signs, and still keep an eye on the white car made her driving chaotic, but by the time she had reached Lake Pontchartrain, she had the route committed to memory.

In her mind, she repeatedly told herself, *Take Claibourne exit, then elevated expressway. Keep to left and exit on Highway 23. Go left under the expressway.*

The white car still followed threateningly behind, and she

prayed for no flat tires or engine trouble. The dark mysterious lake that now stretched out on both sides of her didn't placate her lonesomeness.

In due course the lake ended, and she became confused with the signs. Needlessly she crossed back and forth in the lanes. The car behind distracted her. All at once she saw what she thought was her exit, rushed to take it, and realized too late she had erred. No longer on the Interstate and totally lost, she tried to correct the mistake and ended up in a rough looking section of town. The bridge she should be on was above and behind her now. The white car had followed her off and hesitated even while she hesitated.

A pedestrian leaned against a light post half a block away. She drove straight to him—something she would never have done under normal circumstances. Disreputable looking, heavily whiskered, and dirty, he was at her window before she had totally stopped her truck.

"Where do you want to go?" he asked as if he had done the same many times before.

"I need to cross the Mississippi and get on Highway 23."

He became the friendly neighborhood travel agent and gave brief but sufficient instructions for reentering the Interstate. She handed him a dollar and thanked him.

"I think it's worth more than that," he insisted, his hands still on her windowsill. She realized, then, that this man made his living off lost travelers, the ones who chose the wrong lane and ended up in this run-down area. She handed him a five and rolled her window up, but the man wanted no trouble. He backed away satisfied, and she was thankful his greed had limits.

She turned her truck and hoped she could trust his directions because the white car still followed. Certain now that it had something to do with Mr. Webb and the marijuana growers, she expected the driver to try something before she got out of that quarter, but the car kept its distance.

The remainder of the trip proved easy. When the neon sign of Cody's motel appeared, she pulled in greatly relieved, and the white car passed by without slowing. If only Cody had finished work. She knew his room number and went directly to it.

Noting the light in the room, she knocked and waited tensely.

Shortly the door opened wide, and a shirtless occupant of about thirty with a decidedly French look, stepped into the opening. Upon seeing her, his smile spread all over his face, even his eyes registered geniality.

"Ma'am, were you looking for me?"

"I came to see Cody Strickland. I'm his fiancée. Do I have the right room?"

"I'm Chris." He took her hand and gave a lingering handshake, still smiling. "He's been . . . and gone. . . . and you've missed him. He went to eat . . . or something. I can tell you how to find him, I think, or you can wait a few minutes and follow me." His slight shyness didn't hamper his flirty manner.

"Thank you. I'll wait for you. I'm in no hurry."

"You can come in if you like. We have chairs . . . beds."

"Thank you, but I'll wait in my truck."

Chris left the door open anyway and came out in less than five minutes. Pulling his shirt on as he closed the door behind him, he climbed into an ancient car constructed half of rust and half of black-primed rust.

"I'll go slow. Stay close. I don't want to lose you in the area where we're headed."

"Thank you. I've already been lost in a bad place once tonight. I'll stay right on your bumper."

The smile spread over his face again. "I don't have a bumper."

She followed him closely and hoped they would find Cody. With firm resolution, she pulled off her engagement ring and clenched it tightly in her palm, finally sure about what she should do. Ever since she and Cody had decided on a lifetime together, she had been wavering. It had taken the *Reggie* woman to make her admit something was wrong, *everything* was wrong. It had been painful to find that woman there at Reginald's house, and it *shouldn't* have been. That pain, alone, had shown her that a lifetime with Cody wouldn't work. She realized, at the same time, that she must curb her thoughts and emotions that had been shifting in Reginald's direction. He couldn't be for her either, though for different reasons.

Now she would be alone again, as she had been when Cody first came into her life. He had been a bright spot, likable and funny, and had seemed so right. When he suggested marriage, she had realized that their lifestyles and goals might conflict, but she felt big enough to change and adapt. Now she had reached the point where she didn't *want* to change, and she knew that they couldn't live happily together unless she turned her personality upside down—an acrobatic feat she simply couldn't perform, not gracefully, not at all. She finally admitted to herself that even loneliness outstripped Cody's company.

And then there was the matter of *love*. Where had it gone, or had it ever existed at all—for either of them? She regretted that she had neither understood love's demanding nature nor realized its absence sooner. It would hurt to break up with him and give back his ring. It would hurt her *and* Cody, and maybe their friends and his family, but she mustn't weaken now.

Chris pulled into a sleazy bar. If judged by the almost filled parking lot and the countless patrons who sauntered in and out, it was a popular nightspot. She felt uncomfortable as she followed Chris into the dimly lit building, which almost shook with the vibrations of raucous merriment and loud music.

Cody sat at a table with two women and another man. His arm hung around the shoulders of the woman next to him, and they both laughed about something. He didn't see Jane and Chris's zigzag approach through the narrow lanes between tables.

"I've brought your fiancée, Cody. Hand my girl over now," Chris said laughingly—as quick as he was chivalrous—and put his arm around the girl even as Cody's arm dropped limply away.

"Let's burn up the floor, Pat." Chris pulled her to her feet, and she giggled and followed him to the dance area.

Jane mentally applauded Chris's quick thinking and loyal effort to protect Cody from trouble. The girl, Pat, wasn't as quick but was being carried along anyway. Chris danced well, though a mite on the flamboyant side. Seemingly loose all over, he swayed to the music dreamily. Pat moved clumsily, maybe from too much alcohol, and constantly got caught up in her own feet, but Chris didn't appear to notice. He oscillated around the room with eyes closed and cheek tight against his half-willing partner's cheek.

Cody recovered from his surprise and pulled Jane to the

vacated chair. He dutifully kissed her on the cheek.

"Cody, I can't stay long. I do need to talk with you a minute though. Could we go outside?"

"Sure," he said jovially, but his face held a questioning expression. "Did you drive all that ways by yourself?"

"I enjoyed the drive, except for feeling tired. I haven't slept much lately."

"There's probably still a vacancy at my motel. Let's go there, and I'll get you a room," he said as soon as they left the club.

"I need to go back home tonight—I just had to see you."

"I've missed you too," he said amorously, as if on cue.

"Cody, I *haven't* missed you. That's the trouble." She handed him the ring while tears started to blur her eyes. She hated to hurt anyone and felt wicked clear through. If only she had known her heart and mind sooner.

"Jane, I wasn't cheating on you. Pat and I were just funning around. She's friendly with everyone." His feelings of guilt were embarrassingly obvious.

"It's nothing to do with . . . with *this.*" She waved her hand toward the club in a broad gesture. "We're not right for each other, Cody. We should have been good friends—but it should have gone no further."

"What about my family? What will Bill and Marcia think?"

"We'll tell them we decided not to get married."

"We could stay engaged and not set a date. Wait longer to get married."

"No. I'm certain about this."

She found no way to remain firm and still not wound his feelings.

"Come back inside for a while. You're just tired and angry."

"Cody . . . I'm not angry at all. I made this trip to give you back your ring. I didn't feel right about breaking our engagement over the phone or in a letter. I felt I owed you this much. I simply don't care for you in the way a wife should care for her husband."

Without another word, Cody turned his back and walked back to the club. She watched until he melted into the club's revelry. Tears flowed down her cheeks.

"Now what will I do?" she said aloud. She couldn't remember the twisting, turning route that Chris took, and she couldn't go back in and ask Cody. Maybe the bartender could tell her how to get back to the Interstate. She got into her truck to dry her face and get her composure back, and still sat there forty minutes later, staring out through the windshield at nothing.

A loud tap on her side window so completely startled her that she jumped sideways in her seat. When she turned and saw Reginald's face at the window, anger and relief equally consumed her. What was he doing there? She looked at him a second time to make sure her eyes weren't playing tricks. He motioned her to roll down the window.

"You plan to sit here all night? This establishment will close before dawn. It probably becomes deuced lonely around here. Are you waiting for Cody?"

"No, Cody was called away, and I'm going home, but I'm lost. I planned to ask directions. I . . ."

"You're found now. Hop out. I'll drive you home."

"I can't leave my truck here."

"Harris came with me. He'll drive it back." He reached in and got her keys. "I'm not taking any chances with you this time." He scowled and looked impatient, and she felt too tired to argue.

"I probably should add some oil first," she said resignedly as Harris got in her truck. "And please be aware the brakes and steering don't work well." She got a quart of oil from the back, but Reginald took it from her.

"Get in my car. Harris will know what to do."

Reginald looked unbending as he slid into the seat beside her. Buckling his seat belt, he pressed the button that locked her door.

"I'm still angry, Jane," he said as he pulled out.

She ignored him and stared out the window at the trashy neighborhoods piled one against the other between them and the Interstate. She wouldn't relish driving alone through any of them at night. She glanced at Reginald's face as he studied the road ahead. Possibly she merited his anger. She *had* goaded him with José's information, but she would make no apologies. She didn't intend to talk with him at all.

For a while, she relished the peaceful quiet and watched the miles roll by. Thoughts came and went. Cody hadn't cared enough, and this man annoyed her because he cared too much about everything, and he had no right. The nerve of him to think he could send her on a cruise to get her out of his hair. Her temper freshened. She tried to see his expression again without turning her head in his direction.

"They know who you are, Jane," he said, intruding on the silence. "We did some checking and located one of your Panama City buyers. Webb, or someone, had just called him, and he had obligingly given out your name and address. He thought he'd done you a favor and found you extra work."

"Nice of him, but it doesn't matter. I figured they knew. Someone followed me all the way to Cody's motel."

"Someone followed you all the way to Cody's club too. A white car?"

"Yes."

"Jim drove it. He works for Harris. I set him on your tail when you hung up on me. I had to make sure you were safe, and I needed to know where to find you."

"You had me followed?" She felt so incensed she could hardly talk straight. "You can't even . . . t-take care of yourself! You walk up to marijuana growers and ask about their crops. Y-you write checks for what could be stolen goods. You can't tell the difference between a homemade business card and a printed one, and . . . and . . . you fall out of boats! I should hire a detective to follow *you*!"

"And what would you pay him with, *toads*?"

"Stop and let me out. I'll drive my own truck home. Call Harris. . . . My phone's in my truck."

"You mean *my* phone's in your truck."

He stepped on his accelerator and hummed to himself. She grabbed for his phone, but he reached it first and put it in his pocket. She was so furious she couldn't think of anything sensible to say.

"If you were so worried, why didn't *you* follow me?"

"Why Jane, I had work to do. I don't always have time to play around. I'm a publisher, not a writer. That's why I hired Harris to handle things. And I *did* follow you, later."

"Do you know what it's like to be tailed for two hundred miles by some unknown assailant whom you expect to drive up beside you at any moment and shoot you?"

"I'm glad to know you have *some* feelings of fear, anyway. I'm sorry that Jim frightened you. He called and told me you were aware of his tailing you, but you left us no alternative. You turned off the phone I *loaned* you, and I figured it was better to have you scared than dead. Come to think of it, a bit of fear probably did you good."

He looked over at her, saw her rage, and laughed.

"You couldn't be half as angry as I am, Jane. You went back to see José, alone. That was your second time to go back in there—alone. I won't let you get away with it, Jane, not this time. I'll not give you a chance to hang up on me again either."

"Are you always this charming with women?"

"With women, I'm charming! With ragamuffin snake catchers . . ."

"I'm tired, and I haven't eaten anything all day. Since I'm forced to sit beside an ungrateful monster, do you think you could let me sleep for a while? Us red-necks have to do that now and then, even if highfalutin publishers can get by without it."

"*We* rednecks, would be the correct wordage. And I slept on the way over. Harris drove. Do you want to stop and eat?"

"No, just sleep."

"You can climb in the back if you like."

"I know I can, but right here will do fine." She leaned her head against the window and closed her eyes. She felt him take hold of her hand and squeeze it. She remembered there was no longer a ring there with its promise of love and care and . . . protection. . . . Loneliness swept over her, and she fell asleep.

Much later, she jolted awake when he stopped to get gas at a service station.

"Almost home, Jane. Let's find a place to eat."

"I don't need food. I just need a shower and a change of clothes," she said and straightened in the seat.

"You look fine. Let's eat." He pulled into an all-night restaurant.

"You eat. I'll eat later."

He pulled back out and didn't say a word. She felt guilty for holding a grudge, but he obviously still held his anger too.

"May I make a suggestion?" she asked, though she still looked straight ahead. "Since you're bent on throwing money away right and left, on cruises and detectives and whatever, why don't you do something about this car?"

"What's wrong with my car?"

"It's too noticeable, too memorizable. At this point you should use more care."

He didn't act as if he'd heard, but fifteen minutes later he pulled into an airport and stopped at a car rental agency. Shortly he came out with a set of keys.

"Jane, drive my car and follow me over to the airport's long term parking. I rented a car."

When he pulled out in a flashy white Cadillac, she groaned. The man was hopeless.

Chapter 10

A kiss can hide two faces.

"While we're here at the airport, let's get some breakfast. We highfalutin publishers need to eat every now and then, even if you *writers* don't," he said as he opened the door and helped her out.

They walked together through the short term parking garage across from the terminal and were approaching the street when she suddenly pulled him to a stop. She threw her arms around his neck and drew him close.

"It's Webb. Coming from the terminal. Act like we're lovers saying goodbye," she whispered hastily in his ear.

The words had hardly been said when his arms came tight around her back and his hands crushed into her ribs and waist. He found her startled lips and devoured them while one hand came up and slid into the soft curls at the back of her head.

She jerked back. "Reg!"

"Play your part."

"You're Frenching!"

He cut off her words, and she never knew where Mr. Webb had gone until Reginald turned them both around so he could follow the man's progress.

"He's getting into a cab. Let's follow him," Reginald said in eager huskiness.

They ran for his car and were on their way in minutes, but other drivers hindered their progress, and they lost sight of the cab.

"We missed that one, Jane, but at least he didn't recognize us." He got out his phone and dialed Harris. "Where are you now?"

"Coming into Panama City."

"Park out of sight behind my house. I'll probably be there ahead of you."

When Reginald pulled into his drive, he looked over at Jane.

"Let's wait inside. I can have something fixed for us to eat."

"I haven't time right now. I need to leave as soon as Harris gets here with my truck."

She absolutely couldn't face that Reggie woman the way she looked and felt right then, especially not after that kiss. Would she ever be able to forget that kiss, that innocent, harmless, meaningless, oh-so-meaningful kiss?

"You just got through telling me *my* vehicle was too recognizable. What about your perforated pile of scrap metal? I need you to come in and tell me everything you know, help us get this mystery worked out. Come in, Jane."

That instant Harris and Jim both pulled in behind the house. Reginald walked over and took Jane's truck keys. He casually dropped them into his pocket.

"Do you two want to come in with Jane and me? We need to go over everything."

"Let's go to my office, Reg. I can work better from there. I'll need to check on more things. Glad you changed cars. Park it behind my office."

Jane breathed a sigh of relief and without protest got back into Reginald's car. At Harris's office she recounted her meeting with José and told Harris about seeing Webb at the airport.

"I could recognize this Webb anywhere. Maybe I could go to all these plants and look over their higher-ups. Since you have this detective agency, couldn't you find me some sort of cover," Jane suggested helpfully to Harris.

"Not a chance, Jane," Reginald broke in.

Harris smiled and replied, "You saw the man here today. He may not go back to his business, or his home, until he's done his damage. Right now he's probably looking for you."

"Maybe I could let him find me. That way you could learn

his identity."

"And you could end up like Victor," Harris warned.

"I meant we'd take precautions, of course. I could wait at my house, and someone could watch it or even wait inside with me."

Harris's smile got broader, but Reginald scowled.

"Jane, have you gone mad. That would be a crazy scheme."

"It might work," Harris said, "but it would be better to find him first. He might not take the bait, and we're short on time."

"Maybe he can't report the marijuana yet because he's not sure how much I know. I'm an unknown factor that could mess up his plan. He probably needs to find me," Jane added.

"He probably does, but let's try to find *him*. We haven't located the dentist yet, or else he hasn't had his tooth fixed. If we could learn which factory was involved, we could report a chemical abuse at the place. That might tie his hands and maybe even get him out of the way completely. He probably wants to stop Victor's book to hide some criminal practice, but if he's already charged with the abuse, he no longer has reason to be concerned about the book."

"Everything has to happen by Friday night, or *on* Friday night." Reginald reminded.

Harris looked concerned. "Webb could be a hired henchman, someone lower in the company, or not in the company at all, but I'm gambling on not more than one other person being involved in that part of the scheme. There's been a murder. Few people can handle that or have the stomach to hire it done."

"Could there still be fingerprints on any of the office goods I purchased?"

"I doubt it, but we can check."

"Can't we go to the places we suspect and see if they have white vans?" Jane asked. "Reginald might recognize the van if he saw it up close."

"We've done that already, Jane. We didn't find the van, but then we haven't checked *all* the places yet. It might also be parked somewhere else. Let's study those pictures again from Victor's book."

Jane examined them for the second time—shots of belching smoke stacks, pipes seeping chemicals into waterways, leaking drums of toxic waste, and polluted areas of land and water. Victor had taken a few pictures of entire plants, usually at sunrise or sunset, showing small patches of rosy sky peaking out from clouds of heavy factory smoke. Some of the plants had cars parked at them and an occasional person visible in the parking lot. In one picture a woman looked directly at the camera, obviously curious about the photographer, and another picture showed a man half turned toward the camera preparing to get into his car. A number of people filled the parking lot in a third picture.

She studied the people, seeking the shape or face of Webb, but no one struck her that way. Still, they had been shot at a distance, and she couldn't be sure.

"Maybe you could blow up some of these pictures with people and cars in them."

"I intended to do that. We'll check tag numbers too. One of these long shots could pay off. We're also searching for that Teaman account, using different spellings of the name. That part doesn't make sense yet, but it could eventually implicate Reg in some roundabout way. We have to stay on the lookout for anything. Someone may try to hide evidence in Reg's office or home to make him look more involved," Harris said thoughtfully, "or they could have done it already."

"Or they could leave it on his mutilated body when they dump it in his marijuana fields," Jane said sweetly.

Reginald suddenly lost his steeliness and laughed heartily, which caused everyone else to laugh too.

"Just like the good old days," he said when he gained control, and Jane was afraid to ask him about any more of his good old days.

"At this point, Reg, you and Jane should stay out of the picture until we learn more. Better let us handle the matter now. The perpetrator, or perpetrators, might not wait until Friday."

"You could take that cruise, Reginald, if you still have the ticket," Jane reminded.

"Yes, that's exactly what I need. I can see the headlines: Local drug dealing publisher caught escaping to Caribbean," and he couldn't help but laugh again. Finally, he looked at Jane soberly.

"Jane, you should stay at my house. It's . . ."

"It's the place where they'd expect to find you or stash more evidence. Or they might burn it to the ground. I believe I'd rather pick my own hiding place. Besides, I have schools scheduled this week. I have to show reptiles and amphibians at schools downstate. I might do some collecting and photography in the area too. I'll probably be gone a few days, and I need to leave shortly. I'll have my . . . *your* . . . telephone with me, and if you need me, I can come right back."

"You'll probably be safer away from here," Harris said. "Go ahead, but keep in touch, and when you leave, make doubly sure no one follows."

"How soon will you leave?" Reginald asked worriedly.

"I have to go to my house for a few things, and I'll leave directly from there."

"Jane, if you need something, buy it. I'll cover all expenses."

"I have to pick up the reptiles that I use for my presentations. I don't keep them in my truck, you know."

"I'll pick them up. Tell me what you need."

"I have to do it myself. I have to put them in exhibition cages, and I have to feed and water some of them. You wouldn't know what to do."

"Reg, let Jim take her out there. It will give him a chance to investigate whether anyone has been in her house during her absence."

While waiting for Jim to get ready, Jane stepped into the next room and used the cell phone.

"Marcia, I wanted you to know that I won't be home for a while. I have two school presentations in Ocala, and I may be gone for a few days."

"I'm sorry about you and Cody. Are you sure, Jane?"

"Absolutely sure." Jane hadn't expected Marcia to know already.

"Cody's all broken up about it. He talked to Bill on the phone last night and said you were angry with him for dating another girl. He swore she was only a friend."

"Cody's a friendly sort. The breakup had nothing to do with the girl. Cody and I have grown apart. I don't think either one of us cares much."

"Cody's crazy about you, Jane. He told Bill so."

"Then why did he go fishing without me on Saturday and go out to the clubs Friday night without me? We hadn't seen each other for two weeks. We were engaged, Marcia, not married. What would it be like a year from now? He's already bored with me."

"I don't know, Jane. I guess Bill never acted like that, and he's still pretty good about most things."

"Believe me, Marcia, Cody's not that broken up."

After Jane finally said goodbye, she wondered if she could maintain her friendship with Marcia on the same level as before. Marcia and Bill had been Cody's friends before they became hers. Cody introduced her to them. This split with Cody would no doubt change many things.

Jim drove fast, but when he reached her neighborhood, he cautiously looked the area over before pulling into her drive. Once inside, they both made a careful check of the house.

"Nothing looks amiss. Give me a minute, and I'll get what I need."

She quickly packed a suitcase and got her animals from the shed while Jim continued his work.

"Do you have room in your trunk for this other stuff? I'll need to put the displays on your back seat or the animals will die from the heat."

"That's fine—if they're caged." He laughed nervously.

"They're all secure, and harmless to boot."

"Too bad my kids can't see them. They love that sort of thing."

"Children generally show more enthusiasm for them than adults do."

Jane finished loading, and they left without further fuss.

"Did anyone check what flights had arrived at the airport this morning?" Jane asked as they drove back to the city.

"I checked. Judging from the time Reg said you were there, most likely this Webb came from either the Orlando area or Jacksonville."

"I don't think Victor mentioned any places near Jacksonville, but Orlando is directly in the mid-state area where Victor worked last. It looks like our suspicions have been right. That narrows it somewhat, doesn't it?"

"Not as much or as quickly as we need," Jim reminded her.

At Reginald's house, Jim helped her move everything to her own vehicle.

"We don't know if Webb's seen your truck, but pretend he has," Jim advised. "Be especially cautious until you're away from Panama City. If you think someone's following you, it won't be us. Call us and go straight to the police. Whatever you do, don't stop, not even to ask directions. Webb has to be desperate at this point."

When she headed out of the city, Jane wanted to kick herself. She was still carrying around the check that Reginald hadn't signed. Luckily, she had a couple of schools booked. The small fee she charged would be more than welcome since her tiny reserve of money shrank to a dismal amount in the last week. There would be no motel rooms this trip, but she had other plans for her nights anyway. She had brought the list of suspect plants and meant to do research on her own.

When she stopped for something to eat, she made a list of what she meant to accomplish during the next few days. She had scheduled a school for Wednesday morning and another for early Wednesday afternoon. That would leave plenty of time to investigate, and she would be near the area where Victor had worked.

She studied the plants and factories list, marking the ones located reasonably near the Orlando airport. Only nine of the businesses named in Victor's book would be closer to the Orlando airport than to other large airports. Five of those places were only names in his book with nothing said about them and no pictures. That left four possibilities, and Victor had photographed three of those extensively. Out of those three, two had the same owner. Those two plants seemed most suspect.

It wasn't likely she would come up with anything Harris hadn't already covered, but he couldn't go everywhere and do everything. She might see something if she snooped around, and she could keep her collecting gear with her in case anyone approached her. Her imminent reptile book would make a plausible excuse unless someone caught her spying inside a building.

She could look over one place that evening—the least likely

of the four. Victor had taken no pictures of it, and it was further from the suspect area, but it wasn't far from her schools. After she checked it out, she could drive to her schools and get a good night's sleep before classes started in the morning. At least she wouldn't waste the first night and could gain investigative experience.

Some daylight remained when she arrived at the Tagland Paper Mill. It sat on a sizable piece of ground, but industrial facilities on each side of it left no area where she could pretend to collect. She remembered the problems Victor had mentioned regarding this operation, but he had also said they were improving conditions.

From the number of cars parked in their parking lot, it looked as if they had a small night shift. She drove in as if she were a worker and parked her car with the other vehicles. No one approached her to ask what business she had there, so she sat and watched for a while.

Finally, she concocted a story to use in an emergency, and ventured forth to look around. She walked confidently and searched for white vans or anything else that could be of interest. No one questioned her presence. A few people glanced her way and one of the truck drivers was disposed to be friendly when she passed by him.

"Hot tonight, isn't it. We could sure use a breeze," he said from his seat on the edge of a loading dock.

She cordially agreed and moved on before conversation could ensue. When she came to an open door, she grew braver and stepped into a large, almost empty room with high ceilings and cement floor. The few, scattered people in the building took no notice of her. She studied the interior, unsure of what she hoped to find. At least she was making the acquaintance of paper mills, and that would help since she had another paper mill yet to visit.

When she started to leave, a tall man in a white, short-sleeved shirt walked over to her. He looked like a manager or someone in authority.

"Can I help you?"

"I'm afraid not—guess I'm too late. I was supposed come an hour ago but got held up. She must have gotten a ride with someone else. Thank you anyway. Goodnight."

She left at once and gave him no opportunity to question her further, but she felt discouraged that she had accomplished nothing.

If she could do no better than that, she might as well not waste her time. While driving to the school, she breathed deeply of the fresh air. Not used to paper mill fumes, she had developed a headache in just the short time there.

Later that night she reached her next morning's assignment—a small elementary school. She climbed into the back of her truck to sleep. She had built a full-length box on each side of her truck bed for storage and now used the lid of one of those for a makeshift bed. It was hard and uncomfortable but longer, cooler, and more private than the cab.

After an hour of tossing and turning in the unbearable heat, she opened the back of the topper. Although someone might chance by and see her in there, coolness seemed preferable to safety on a night so stifling. She spent the rest of the night undisturbed and by early morning felt ready for the work and risks ahead.

The presentations went smoothly, and the keen interest of the students always made it an enjoyable task. By two o'clock in the afternoon, she had finished both of the scheduled schools and immediately called Harris's detective agency. She wanted news and was sure Reginald wouldn't give her any. Surprisingly, Harris answered her call.

"Jane, you're giving Reginald a fit. He's called you a dozen times this morning."

"I can't talk on my phone while I'm presenting school programs."

"He'd think you could."

"Yes, I know he would. Has anything new happened since I've been gone?"

"Still checking tag numbers, dentists, snake ladies—a little of everything."

"Harris, could that cargo van have been a rental? Webb *flew* to Panama City that last time. Maybe he rented one."

"Jim's looking into that. I'll let you know if he learns anything."

Unthinkingly, she had almost revealed that the white van had come to mind while she checked a paper mill. She must watch what she said or Reginald would have a detective on the hunt for her again.

"Will you call Reginald and tell him I'm fine? I plan to collect now, and I probably won't have the phone turned on."

"I'll tell him, but that won't stop him from calling."

"Is someone keeping an eye on him? I don't think he realizes his danger. He doesn't seem to *think* about danger."

"It's hard to hold him down, Jane. He's almost as bad as you."

"Well, no one has to worry about me."

"Don't we now?" he asked so suspiciously, she feared he knew her plans.

Chapter 11

Bent ladders can lead to crooked schemes.

The plant she intended to investigate that night lay further south—another paper mill. She decided to save the two most likely plants until the next day when she would have plenty of time for a more careful examination.

This mill rested in a nicer setting, out in the country with orange groves on every side of it, but it still spewed out the nauseating smoke associated with paper companies. She wondered if it affected the nearby oranges. The heavy odor in the air must surely permeate everything nearby, including the crops.

She found no nearby place to park, and the groves wouldn't do because someone might think she parked there to steal oranges. She must risk parking at the mill again. At least plenty of cars filled the parking lot, but the present shift could get off at any time. Hopefully another shift followed this one.

At least her truck resembled most of the other vehicles there, old and tired looking. She felt sorry for the people who earned their living at the smelly facility. Whatever their pay, it should be raised, she told herself.

It had just turned three o'clock, too early to investigate the mill. Now that Webb could identify her, she must work in darkness. Rather than endure a long, hot wait in her truck, she decided to check for reptiles in the groves. She wouldn't likely find any, considering all the chemicals that groves used, but she could at least spy on the factory from a safe distance. Already dressed in her collecting clothes, she slid a small knife, her cell phone, and a few other items into her pocket and laced some reptile bags through her belt. She left the rake and camera behind this time.

Her animals presented somewhat of a problem because of the intense afternoon heat and no fresh air blowing in like when she drove. Having no other options, she draped wet bags over the cages and left the topper windows and the topper back partially open for cross ventilation, but locked the cab. Cautiously she followed the factory's low, chain-link fence halfway to the road in front of the mill and quickly stepped over into the grove.

Keeping within sight of the fence, she headed toward the back of the grove on the chance it might open into fields or woods good for collecting. Though she stayed far enough into the grove for the trees to hide her, she could still see the loading docks of the mill. Soon she came upon a stretch of cross fencing, which separated the front part of the grove from a back area of older growth. Many of the trees in the older section had died, and those that still showed greenery looked as if they no longer produced fruit. Weeds and vines had taken over everything. She noted that the fence lay even with the back of the adjacent mill.

She had seen many old groves like the one she now faced, usually abandoned because the owner couldn't afford the expense of replanting. Citrus entailed much risk in that area of the state. A couple of years of frosts at the wrong time could ruin a grower. She climbed over the fence and proceeded through the older grove in search of specimens. That grove wouldn't have received any recent chemical applications, and nature might have replenished it with animal life. It looked wild and grown up enough to house anything, but the paper mill fumes persisted even there. Her throat grew raw from breathing them, and her head began to pound again. It would be nice just to go home since she didn't know how to investigate anyway, but she did know she had caused new complications and shouldn't leave it all to Reginald. She must at least make an effort.

Soon she came to another fence with more of the same type of grove continuing on the other side of it. This time she didn't climb over but followed it in a direction away from the mill. After a short distance, she came to a narrow limestone drive that would no doubt take her to the highway if she turned left on it. To the right it looked like it led a distant warehouse barely visible through the trees. A locked gate prevented anyone from driving to the building, but she climbed over the fence and walked back to investigate.

The metal building looked old and rusted, and it backed up to yet another fence. Beyond that fence lay a stagnant, swampy area. She checked around the warehouse grounds for animal life. The area should have teemed with lizards and snakes, but she found nothing, not even in the narrow stretch of high weeds between the back of the building and the fence.

Before long she noticed that the building had a stench of its own, as did the boggy area on the other side of the fence behind the warehouse. The bog itself seemed devoid of life. An occasional stump rose out of the stagnant green water, but no turtles rested on any of them, and no birds roosted in the sparse trees. No minnows swam the shallows and not even a water bug scooted across the water's surface. Jane wondered if she had come upon an infringement that Victor had missed, even though he investigated next door to it. He could easily have missed it. Higher land and a grove of older, no longer producing trees totally enclosed the swamp area.

On the far side of the warehouse grounds sat piles of clutter and discarded equipment, including an old tanker and some rusted trucks with weeds grown up around them. In due course, she realized she stared at the name of the paper mill next door. It said "M P Pulp & Paper Co." in faded letters on the side of one truck. A further search brought to light another vehicle with the mill's name emblazoned on it and a truck lettered Greenwood Groves. The two companies must have something to do with each other, possibly belonged to the same man, just like the two plants she planned to investigate on the morrow.

She wanted to look inside the warehouse, but padlocks secured all the entrances, and the corrugated steel walls looked unscalable. Upon further investigation, she discovered an opening on the back of the warehouse between the top of the walls and the roof. The four-foot peak at the center of the roof left plenty of room to enter that way, though maybe only into an attic area. The sixteen foot walls looked intimidating, and she had a healthy fear of heights, but she did want to see inside that building. She went back to the piles of rubble and found a stack of disposed tools, including damaged, aluminum fruit-picking ladders. She took the best of the lot. Chuckling grimly, she wondered if Reginald would bail her out of jail if someone caught her breaking into the place.

The two-foot clearance between the back of the building and the fence caused more difficulty. She had to prop the ladder almost straight up and couldn't help but climb timidly as she stared down at the sea of green scum and contemplated where she might land if the ladder toppled backward. It would be a sloppy landing, but not life threatening unless she landed on a submerged stump. She would probably sink to her waist in slime and chemicals, but that was less scary than a hard landing on cement or rock.

When she climbed high enough to grasp the top of the wall with one hand, she felt the relief only someone with that kind of fear could understand. If the ladder failed, she had a grip on something and wouldn't fall. After climbing three more steps, she peered into the depths below.

The building had no ceiling, just long rows of two-by-ten beams at two-foot intervals stretching from front to back wall. Two large box trucks were housed on one side, and one of them reached within about four feet of those joists. It would be possible to climb over and drop onto it. It also gave her a moderately quick exit if that became advisable.

With a ready means of escape available, she climbed shakily onto the beams. Slowly she scooted and crawled across the long building until the truck lay directly below her. Lowering herself unto it, she made her way forward to the cab and climbed down from there.

Enough light came through the building's roof opening to give some visibility in the unlit warehouse. She examined the vehicles and saw that neither of them had lettering. Their cargo areas were open and empty. When she found the cab unlocked on one, she climbed up into it.

The glove compartment contained only the vehicle registration. With the aid of the small light from the screen of her cell phone, she saw that it was made out to a Maxwell Painter. She copied the pertinent information it contained and continued her search. Under the seat, she found two large magnetic signs lying upside down. They looked like floor mats, and she had almost passed them by. A different name was printed on them—Central Appliance. She noted the information and closed the door.

Marks on the dusty doors of the truck showed that the signs had been placed there recently. She wondered if the owner also owned an appliance business.

She turned her attention to one corner of the building, piled high with large metal drums. Much of the strong chemical smell came from them. Her throat burned from it, and she wished she had brought water with her.

The opposite corner on that side of the building contained an assortment of litter. She pulled back a large piece of mildewed canvas and found a spigot under it, close against the wall in the corner. She wondered if the water was drinkable or if the pipes were old and deteriorated. When a trickle of yellowish fluid came out, she quickly shut off the valve. Stooping to sniff the still dripping faucet, she realized it wasn't water. It had a chemical odor, the same stench as the drums and the swamp behind the building.

A further search of the building turned up an old pop bottle half-full of moldy soda with its screw on cap still intact. Emptying the contents, she filled it with liquid straight from the tap. After she had recapped it and slid it into one of the small collecting bags on her belt, she replaced the canvas exactly as it had been.

When further investigation uncovered nothing of interest, she climbed back onto the joists and made the exhausting climb back to the welcome outside world. One glance at the foul smelling pool below told her she needed a sample of that too.

She returned the ladder to its trash heap and searched for another specimen bottle. There were plenty of pop bottles in the piles of junk, but none had caps. Finally she whittled a stopper from a piece of stick, bottled some of the stagnant liquid, and tucked it away in another bag.

Because she wanted to find the origin of that foul fluid, she decided to check what had most aroused her curiosity—the direction of the pipe connected to the spigot. She found a broken handled shovel in the stack beside the discarded ladders and began to dig at the corner of the building where the spigot was located. If the pipe didn't run back under the warehouse, she should be able to find it.

The ground was hard but workable. At a two-foot depth, she struck the pipe, and by widening the hole could determine its direction. It pointed toward the adjacent mill whose smoke billowed above the line of treetops. Still, it could make a turn at any point and head back toward the front of the grove. She chose a point about fifteen feet away, in line with it direction, and dug a new hole. It took a while to find the pipe again but it was there. She had only gotten off to one side by about a foot.

With the shovel upright in the new hole, for a bearing point, she went back to her original diggings and sighted a far distant spot for a final dig. As soon as she had marked the new spot, she filled both the other holes and tamped them until the ground appeared undisturbed.

She returned to the new spot to make the final, most important check. If the pipe could be located again, she would know for sure it had nothing to do with the grove. It would directly line up with the mill, and nothing lay between except a few scraggly trees.

It took a three-foot-wide trench to find the pipe—still headed in the mill's direction. By the time she had filled that hole and stomped the ground firm, she knew she should leave. She couldn't risk investigating the plant next door, and she needed to call Harris. She hurried through the groves, anxious to leave the area.

Upon nearing the fence beside the mill, she discovered the parking lot had emptied. Evidently they ran no night shift. Her heart jumped when she saw two men standing by her truck. One of the men lifted the back of her topper and stuck his head inside. Jane stepped into the crotch of an orange tree. Hidden by the limbs, she watched to see what they would do. The same man got out a notepad and obviously took down her license number while the other peered through the window of her locked cab.

Just as she prepared to call Harris on her phone and ask his advice, the men turned away and started back toward the plant. Without hesitation, she hurried across the remaining grove and over the fence into the parking lot. With her truck hiding her from view, she ran for the door, jumped in, and left without a backward glance.

Excitedly, she pulled onto the road and dialed Harris as she drove. Almost instantly he answered her call, and she related all she'd discovered and where she was located.

"Jane, don't drive back here. Go to the local police department in that city. I'll call them now, and I'll also call an official with the EPA. You turn over what you collected to the EPA, and we'll let them take care of things. Don't mention the marijuana or the murders. If this is what it appears to be, it's enough of an infraction to send someone to jail. We can pin those murders on them later if it's related."

"You mean murder—don't you?"

"Two murders. Victor and your Mr. Teeman—that's spelled with two e's. We just found out about John Teeman, a state inspector, but forget about that for now. I'll tell you when you get back. It's better if you don't know too much until after you've talked to the EPA. Tell them you're working on a book about hazardous waste dumping, and you had reason to suspect this place. Don't say anything more, and get back here as quick as you can. Please be cautious. Even if someone is jailed, there could be another person involved who won't realize it—like Webb, who's probably still here in our area."

"Yes, I thought of that. The owner of these places must be the Maxwell Painter who's listed on the registration—since the mill is named M P Pulp and Paper, but unless Painter is also Webb, we've still got problems."

"We should know about that directly. Call me when you're near Panama City, and I'll tell you where to go. By the way, did you turn your phone off?"

"I was too busy to take any calls."

"Well, you can imagine Reg's state. He started to go after you three hours ago, but I persuaded him to wait a few minutes longer. Better call him."

"You call him, Harris. Please?"

"Okay, but keep your phone in operation, or I'll go down there myself."

A short while later she met with the three EPA officials. One of them took charge of the bottles while the other two took her statement. They wanted her to remain, but she explained she had to get back home right away.

"You have my cell phone number. If you need to ask me anything further, I'll have it by me day and night."

"We don't know what's in these bottles yet, but it might be a good idea to wash thoroughly before going anywhere," one of the officials advised as he sniffed the contents of a bottle. "It smells potent."

"I don't believe I got any on me except on my hands. If I can use the washroom here, I should be fine. Thank you and good luck. I hope I've not wasted your time."

"It doesn't sound like a false alarm, and that's our job—to check out every suspicion."

Chapter 12

These are the times that try men's souls.

A half-hour on her way back, Reginald called. He acted *too* nice. She recognized his efforts to suppress his anger and lure her back into his clutches.

"Exemplary work, Jane."

He paused, and that pause told her more than his words of praise had revealed. He wore his feelings too much on the outside—on his face and in his voice. No, he wasn't a good liar. She grinned to herself because she knew very well how he felt right then.

"Reginald, this evidence I've found could prove to be nothing, and it may not relate to your problem. Can you tell me about Teeman now?"

"Teeman worked for the state and inspected places like this mill you investigated. Evidently he went there regularly. Harris and I enlarged all of Victor's pictures, including the ones of M P Pulp and Paper. We checked the cars in the parking lot whose license numbers we could make out. Remember the car with a man getting into it, the one where the man looked partway around toward the camera?"

"A blue car?"

"*That* car is registered to John Teemam, and the police found John Teeman in his blue car in a bad section of Jacksonville, shot in the head by a small caliber gun at close range—and robbed to boot. They found him late at night on the same day that Victor took that picture."

"I see, and Victor took that picture early in the day. Why Jacksonville?"

"That's where Teeman lived. The police haven't released any information yet, but Harris and I think Teeman was murdered that morning and not in Jacksonville. Forensics should bear up our suspicions. We don't know the identity of the man entering his car, but it's definitely not Teeman. We have a picture of him now and can confirm that fact anyway. We have to assume that the man in that picture murdered Teeman, and Victor probably photographed him immediately after doing the deed."

"How terrible!" She shivered when she thought of Reginald involved in such a situation.

"In any case, Victor caught the murderer by surprise, exactly at the second he got into Teeman's car to take it and the body to Jacksonville. The three pictures Victor took directly before that one show different sides of the same mill. He had probably moved around to the parking lot side to get another angle. I'm sure he had no idea of what he'd just photographed."

"If the murderer drove Teeman's car to Jacksonville, how would he follow Victor home? He wouldn't drive all the way to Panama City first, not with a body in the car, and how would he pick his car up from the mill?"

"He no doubt drove to the mill with someone else, possibly this Webb. There must be at least two people handling this, considering how much was done and how quickly."

"Don't start feeling secure," Jane warned. "You don't have a picture of Max Painter yet. If he doesn't look like Webb *or* the man standing by the car, that could indicate that you have the wrong place, or the wrong man, or that more men are involved."

"I don't think so. If they find criminal abuse at his mill, that should confirm our hunch, especially since Teeman inspected for that sort of infringement."

"Reginald, you are forgetting that Lubin and Tomás probably don't know anything about this, and they might not be as amiable as José."

"Where are you now?" he asked, changing the subject.

"Between Ocala and Gainesville."

"When you get back tonight, we'll have a bit of a chat about this stuff. Come straight to my house."

She saw through him instantly. He acted friendly, even shared information with her, and now he pretended he needed to discuss evidence with her so he could get his hands on her and keep her from further involvement. She remembered how he enticed her back the last time by hinting he knew something about the tooth. The man couldn't be trusted.

"I'm awfully sleepy. I may get a motel room and wait until morning to start back. I could meet you at Harris's later in the day."

"Dash it all, Jane, drink some coffee, and wake up. Get on back here. I need your help. It's still early."

"Two days ago you wanted me to stay away, 'take a cruise,' you said."

"To the blooming Caribbean—that's where I wanted you. Now you're in Florida, where I don't want you." His exasperation had gotten the best of him.

"You're house sits in Florida, Reginald, and you just asked me to meet you there. I'll be asleep soon. Try not to call unless it's important."

She hung up and knew he would call again as soon as he had his control back. Within a few minutes, the phone rang. Gritting her teeth, she took it up.

"Yes."

"Miss Pate? I'm the EPA officer you just talked with, Ronald Pullman. I thought you might be interested to know we confirmed your hunch. Both bottles tested toxic, especially the one from the spigot—raw waste. We believe someone piped it directly there and either poured it into the ground or transported it elsewhere in one or both of those trucks. Those magnetic signs were obviously decoys to protect the driver when he made an illegal dump. No such appliance company exists in this area—never has. We have men at the warehouse now, and we'll make arrests shortly."

"Thank you for letting me know so quickly. Did you notify the gentleman that called you about it—Mr. Bair?"

"Mr. Bair at the detective agency? Yes, one of our agents is on the line with him right now."

She sighed happily after the call ended. They had notified Harris, and He would contact Reginald and save her from that task. They would apprehend the criminals and she could put her other blunders behind her. Even if they didn't catch all of them, the others would disappear. They had no reason to frame Reginald now. Poor José might get into trouble. He wasn't a criminal, just a naive, unthinking boy following his brother. Maybe his brother was likable and naive too. She felt bad for both of them.

She found a motel on the outskirts of Gainesville, and after a shower and some dinner, she called Harris and gave him her location. Before she could say goodbye, Reginald came on the line.

"Did you hear the news, Jane?"

"About the pending arrest?"

"Not pending. They've done it. They've arrested the owner of the plant, this Max Painter, though he hasn't admitted anything yet. They faxed us his picture upon our request. He's not Webb or the man getting into the car, but those two may be thugs that Painter hired. We told the police about Teeman and sent them a copy of the picture with Teeman's car in it so that they'd know what his supposed murderer looks like. We've also told them our suspicions about Victor's death, and about his book and pictures. We *haven't* told anyone about Webb or the Marijuana yet. We'll do that soon though."

"Please be watchful. Two murderers may still be on the loose, and it might be business as usual with them."

"Between the EPA and the police, they will certainly be located."

"Great. I can get a good night's sleep then. See you tomorrow."

She did sleep extremely well, but not until she had locked and bolted the door and placed a chair in front of it. Nine hours later, she awoke to bright daylight streaming between the curtain tiers. The hot day had begun early. She slid into old khaki shorts and an olive tank top—the last of her clean clothes.

Yesterday's clothes resided in a plastic bag, which she threw into the back of her truck on the chance they might be contaminated. She scrubbed her boots in the bathtub and tossed them into the back too. For lack of anything better, she put on an old pair of crew socks and some lace-up boots she always kept with her for spares.

At Tallahassee, she made a side trip to see one of her buyers, just in case he had collected some unusual specimen she could photograph for her book. They talked and time slipped by. When she finally arrived at Harris's, it was after two.

"Hey, Jane, you just missed Reginald. I hoped you'd stay in Gainesville another day until we cleared up everything.

"Have they apprehended anyone besides Painter yet?"

"Not yet, but they say they're close. Painter hasn't talked. He claims to know nothing about any of this. Reginald went to take care of a few things, and then we'll tell them about the rest of the stuff—Webb, the frame, the marijuana, everything."

"What are the 'things' he went to take care of?"

"He didn't say. Probably wants to give one last check through his papers to see if they planted any evidence to frame him for the Teeman murder other than that check José told you about. He asked me to keep you here until he got back if you arrived while he was gone."

"And did he honestly think you could?"

Harris grinned widely and shook his head helplessly.

"It would be a kindness if you'd stay for a few minutes. I need more information. Maybe you can help me."

"That sounds like Reginald's tactics."

"Okay, here sits a stack of magazines and over there sits the coffee. Stay a while, just in case Reg calls. At least then he can see I tried."

"I'd stay, but I need to do something with my specimens. The sun on my truck will kill them. I should take them home and put them back in their regular cases."

"That would be unwise, Jane. This isn't over yet. Can't you bring them in the back and put them in the storage room? It's empty."

"All right, if you don't mind."

While she brought in the last of them, Harris came back to tell her Reginald had called.

"I told him you would wait here at my office. Please don't make me out a liar—not immediately anyway."

He watched for a while as she fed and watered the specimens

that needed care.

"What's wrong with that snake? What's that enormous bulge in its body. Is it deformed?"

For answer, Jane got out a turtle that measured about five inches long and was almost that broad. She held it up beside the bulge in the snake's body.

"I can't believe that! The snake swallowed a turtle that big? Shell and all? Won't that kill the snake?"

"The bulge will get smaller and smaller as it digests the turtle. Turtles are one of the items on its diet. It got into one of my turtle traps, swallowed the turtle, and couldn't get back out between the wires. I caught it before it found the trap opening."

"Is it poisonous?"

"No, just a water snake."

"I've seen those before—always thought they were moccasins."

"They closely resemble each other."

"Guess I'll keep thinking they're all moccasins—safer that way," he said and left to answer a phone call.

When she finished the task and returned to the front, Cody waited there for her. Harris looked sheepish and tried to appear busy with his papers.

"Jane, Reg told me you'd be here. I need to see you."

"I'm parked in back. I'll meet you back there."

"Come eat with me. We need to talk."

"I don't need to talk, Cody, but I'll have an iced tea with you. There's a place across the way. How about there?"

"All right, Jane."

Instead of getting into his car, she waited for a break in traffic and sprinted across the four lanes. While he ordered, she took a seat and studied him, amazed she felt only relief that she had ended their engagement. She would be sociable, but firm. She doubted she could keep him as a friend after refusing him as a lover, but she would try.

She wondered why Reginald had told him her whereabouts. He usually insulted Cody, but now he sends him right to her doorstep. Did he want her to make up with Cody? Maybe he feared she would pursue *him* now that she and Cody had split. He, of course, belonged to the Reggie woman. Her analysis of the situation left her feeling indignant. How could Reginald think she would go after him? She never did anything to make it look that way, nothing much, anyway. Maybe she, more or less, invited him to go snake hunting with her—alone in the woods with her. She *had* insisted on staying at his office all night to help with his investigations, and then bought him dinner too. And then at the airport . . . She lowered her head and blushed at the thought. Webb had showed up so suddenly, and she could think of nothing else to do. Reginald certainly hadn't hesitated. She started to relive the poignant moment when Cody arrived with their drinks.

"Did you finally get an extra day off work?" she asked and smiled at him.

If only she could avoid a serious conversation. She didn't relish refusing the ring and the man a second time.

"I took a day off. Jane, I've called your house a bunch of times but never reached you. I finally called Reg, and he told me you went down to the middle of the state for school programs. Last night he called and said you'd be back this morning."

"I'm sorry I caused you to miss a day of work. Didn't he give you my cell phone number?"

"Reg said I should see you, and I didn't think you would see me if I asked. So I just came."

"I see."

"Jane, I know I shouldn't have let you drive home alone from that . . . place. It's a bad area, and I let my temper get the best of me. Reg told me . . ."

She waited. When he didn't go on, she anxiously asked, "Reginald told you *what*?"

"It doesn't matter . . . Anyway, I'm sorry."

She realized it did matter to her. Everything about Reginald mattered, and she grew impatient to finish the interview.

"I'm not angry, Cody. I'm only sorry I didn't realize sooner that we weren't right for each other."

"Sure we're right for each other. You're still angry about that girl."

"Cody, I drove to New Orleans to give you back your ring. The girl had nothing to do with it."

"I could have changed your mind if you hadn't seen Pat. You and I always got on fine. Everyone says we're crazy to break up. My family likes you a lot. What about them?"

"What about you? You didn't rush to spend time with me this last weekend, did you?"

"That doesn't mean I didn't miss you."

"You missed me about as much as I missed you. We should have been friends, Cody—just friends. We enjoyed each other's company for a while, had some good times together, but a happy marriage requires more commitment and more love than either of us can offer."

"Go out with me tonight."

He placed his hand over hers, and she felt an unpleasant sensation.

"I'm sorry. I'm very sorry." She pulled away and rose from the table. "I have to go now." She walked out the door, crossed the street, and never looked back.

When she entered the office, Harris was on the phone at the front desk. He glanced at her interestedly for a minute before he gave his attention back to the party on the line.

"No. Definitely not. You guessed that one wrong. I'll talk with you later."

He made no mention to her of the call, but she felt he hid something. The phone rang again, and Jane busied herself with the reptiles until Harris called her.

"They called about Teeman's Alabama bank account. No one knew about it—not even his wife. Evidently he was on the take, probably blackmailed one, maybe more, of the businesses he inspected. It looks like M P Pulp and Paper got tired of paying, or maybe couldn't afford the price tag. Teeman owned a sizable account, which showed regular deposits. Judging from the amounts of those deposits, he bled someone for big money. They also found that a five hundred-dollar check to a Lubin Cruz was paid out of it recently—with a poor imitation of Teeman's signature. I guess Reg better make sure Teeman's checkbook isn't planted anywhere in his home or office."

"Do they know anything yet about who murdered Teeman or Victor?"

"Not yet, but they'll contact me if they learn anything. Now

I need to call Reginald with this news, and then I have to go out for a while—a doctor's appointment. I can't cancel it or my wife will murder me, and there will be a third murder for the police to solve. The office will be empty, but you can stay if you like. I'll come back by here after my appointment. I think it would be best if you stayed at my house tonight."

"I'd like to stay here a few minutes and look at your copy of Victor's book—also the pictures you blew up. I'll probably be here when you get back, but I think I'll check into a motel tonight."

"Make sure you let me know what one." He dialed Reginald's number, waited a minute, and then dialed again.

"You think he's all right?"

"He should be. He just called . . . when . . . a while ago," he finished lamely.

"You mean you were talking with him when I came back from my very short date with Cody, right?"

"He . . . asked if you wore a ring. . . . After all, Jane, I *am* his detective." He grinned guiltily.

"Did he say where he was or where he was going?"

"Only that he'd call back later. If he calls you, or if you reach him, let him know about the Teeman account. Meanwhile, I'll try to reach him and will call you if I'm successful. Also, don't let anyone in here. The people who belong here have keys. Work in my office so you won't be visible if anyone comes to the door."

"I'll be careful. I'm somewhat worried about Reginald, though. Either or both of those men could be somewhere near here, and so might the marijuana planters. You understand my concern, don't you? You *know* Reginald."

"You mean—do I realize he might walk up on all four or five of them and say, 'By Jove, what's the bloody idea of murdering my writer?'"

His fake English accent sounded so much like Reginald, Jane laughed.

"Yes. That's exactly what I mean."

Jean James • Mary James

Chapter 13

One strike and you're out.

  The empty office gave Jane an eerie feeling as she sat alone at Harris's cluttered desk. With no windows in his office, and a small reading lamp offering the only light, the place emanated gloominess. She dialed Reginald repeatedly, but he didn't answer.

  Victor's book lay open before her, and she randomly paged through it. Though she gazed at the pages, she didn't bother to read anything. Reginald filled her thoughts full to overflowing. She wondered why he asked Harris if she wore a ring—no doubt he meant Cody's ring. He not only told Cody where to find her but also reprimanded him and obviously advised him. She wished he would mind his own business, but that was Reginald. He jumped into everything. She smiled to herself, but the smile quickly faded into a worried frown. What was he up to now? Would he act careless or reckless now that the police worked on the case? Was he in danger?

  She studied the book in front of her with closer attention in an effort to get her mind off Reginald. She read again Victor's last pages and realized she had already committed most of them to memory. He had written a compelling book. Maybe Reginald would let her help in its completion.

  Beside Victor's book, lay a stack of his enlarged pictures. She studied them with new interest now that she had personally viewed some of plants. Toxic waste abuse had become real to her. When she studied the pictures of pipes pouring waste into waterways, she remembered the tainted water behind the grove, and when she looked at the blackened smokestacks, she smelled again the stench of paper factory.

Harris had numbered the M P Pulp and Paper mill pictures in the order they were taken. She could follow Victor's steps as he photographed his last scenes and gazed at his last sunrise. The pictures showed off his talent as a photographer. The mill smoke billowed and blended with the colors of the rising sun, both beautiful and terrible at the same time. And that was what Victor had wanted.

When she came to the shot of the mill with Teeman's car in the parking lot, cold chills crept up her back. It was like watching a real murder take place. The supposed murderer had turned enough toward Victor that she could actually look into his eyes. She almost expected to see a spot of blood somewhere or some piece of evidence that would proclaim that a man had just met eternity.

The picture only showed a man climbing into a car not his—a man looking in surprise at a sudden witness to his deed. She studied again the half-turned head and looked into the eyes that the camera had looked into. *She knew who he was*!

She studied him for another instant to make sure. Trembling, she reached for the phone and dialed Reginald. With no answer, she tried to reach Harris and had no luck there either. What should she do? She studied the picture again, more carefully this time. The clothes, the hair, everything jelled. It had to be the same man.

The police were looking for their murderer in the wrong place. They should be investigating the mill she checked that first night, Tagland Paper Mill, the one that none of them suspected. The man's short-sleeved, white shirt jogged her memory. She recognized his face too. Webb might be this man's employee, or maybe his boss, but he must have been there too. Was he the one who followed Victor home, the one who murdered Victor?

A study of the few employee cars parked there showed that one of them had a Marion County tag, which was the location of the Tagland mill. With a magnifying glass from Harris's desk, she examined the Marion car more closely. A man sat in the driver's seat, but he was probably only a worker that lived in that adjacent county. That was common enough. She was wasting time now, grasping at straws.

She leafed through Harris's papers on the suspect factories

and plants and found the sheet that listed the owners. Near the top of the list she found the name—Tagland Mills, owner: Richard Taggart. That meant that either the man getting into the car was Richard Taggart or possibly Webb was Taggart. The man she talked with at the mill that night could easily have been the owner.

Only a couple of minutes had gone by since she called Reginald and Harris, but she tried their numbers again, unsuccessfully. With her patience gone, she left a note explaining to Harris about the man in the picture. She also told Harris that she was going to hunt for Reginald—that Reginald could be in trouble. She signed it and leaned it against the phone. He should be back in the office within minutes, but she couldn't wait any longer. A feeling of calamity washed over her.

Where could Reginald possibly be? she asked herself as she got into her truck. She drove by his office first, but it was dark and no cars were in its parking lot.

She turned around and headed toward his house. She hated to fall under the haughty stare of that woman again, but Reginald needed to know immediately. Realizing there was no need for caution now, she screeched to a halt directly in front of his house. She rang the bell and pounded at the same time. When no answer came, she ran around to the back and looked for cars. The back was deserted too.

With a sinking feeling, she headed out of town. She thought she knew where Reginald went—the place she feared he would go all along—and now she feared the worst. Ignoring speed limits and the danger of hitting a deer at night on that seldom-traveled highway, she headed toward the marijuana fields. She hoped her hunch proved wrong. There was no need to dial Harris again. He would get her note and would probably guess where she went to search for Reginald, but that couldn't be helped. She continuously dialed Reginald as she drove along and prayed she wouldn't find his Cadillac hidden there in the bushes. Maybe he had decided to drive down to the mill and check into things himself. He knew what Webb looked like. Maybe he thought he could help the police find their man.

Even while she tried to convince herself that he went somewhere like that, she knew he would answer her calls if that were so. Finally, she gave up speculation and concentrated solely on driving. She was uncertain what to do if she didn't find his car, and more uncertain what to do if she found it hidden along that road.

When she came to the spot where she had parked the last time, she drove all the way in so her headlights would light the area. The place was empty, and she turned her car back out onto the highway.

Three quarters of a mile down the road sat the spot where they parked for their toad hunt. Because of the darkness, she almost missed the opening and had to backtrack. Entering cautiously, her headlights lit up the gleaming Cadillac.

She leaped from her truck, motor still running, and rushed to his car with flashlight in hand. She envisioned the Teeman car with its body in the front seat, but this car was decidedly empty.

With gritted teeth, she climbed back into her truck, turned it around, and parked it beside his car, facing the exit. Reginald, obviously in the same frame of mind, had pointed his car outward for a quick getaway too. He knew he courted danger.

She slid a long sleeved shirt on over her clothes for protection for her arms, but there wasn't time to do anything about her legs. Her pockets contained only her flashlight, a knife, and cell phone, which she had already turned off. She grabbed her rake for use as a possible weapon and set off across the highway.

Noiselessly she crept in the direction of the shed. Maybe she would find only Reginald there. He might have gone back to look things over, or he might even have gone to take pictures. It *was* late, so maybe none of the others would be there, especially since the meeting wasn't until the next night.

She doubted Reginald would go armed but had to consider it a possibility. She proceeded cautiously so he wouldn't mistake her for the wrong person. If she caught sight of him, and he wasn't in any trouble, she could slip back to her truck and leave before he ever discovered she had come. She could only guess how vehement he would act if he discovered she came there alone again. Yes, by all means, silence was imperative.

The darkness slowed her progress, but she dared not use a light. She felt, rather than saw, the swamp area when she came to it.

With almost no moonlight for guidance, it soon became impossible to keep her feet dry. The lace-ups, though not as protecting for snakebites, at least didn't fill with water or become sucked off in the mud. Long pants would have been a comfort, but it was her hat that she missed most. She constantly had to pull spider webs from her hair and wondered how many spiders had hitched a free ride on her clothes or body. To her, they were scarier than snakes, but at least she couldn't see them in the darkness, and that helped.

Just when she wondered if she had wandered off course, she saw a pinprick of light far ahead and to her left. It looked like lantern light, like the one they used that other night. A cold chill again traveled up her back as she grew more and more fearful for Reginald.

With the utmost caution, she crept in the direction of the light, but kept it on her south side. It disappeared from time to time as obstructions came between her and it, but finally she came close enough to see it clearly. By then she stood in two feet of water, her boots sunken inches into the ooze below. She advanced no further but tried to make out the situation.

She could see three people. They talked, and one gestured excitedly. She heard voices, but she couldn't make out words. Silently she crept behind a large cypress tree. If a flashlight beam traveled in her direction, the tree would hide her totally.

Peering around the trunk, she could now see the scene clearly. She identified Lubin, Tomás, and finally Webb. Had they caught Reginald? If they had, he could be in the shed, or in a boat, or dumped in the water. Her blood chilled at the thought. Her apprehension had turned into terror as she feared she came too late.

Tediously, silently, she crept toward the south. If she could make it to that small branch of water at the end of his property, she could follow it to the river. She could then follow back along the bank of the river and see what boat or boats they brought. She might locate Reginald if he was there—or his *remains*, she thought gloomily.

Her teeth chattered in spite of the warmth of the night. She clenched her mouth tightly and concentrated on the job at hand. She covered about twenty feet when a short distance ahead of her she heard a log snap, followed by a loud splash.

Instantly alarmed, she moved swiftly away from the sound, afraid that history would repeat itself. The three men must have startled a deer or some large animal. Now the sound would lead them right to her. She ducked low and hurried away from the beams of light that suddenly flooded the area. The men ran in the direction of the beams, and she was suddenly horrified to see Reginald struggling to his feet as the first of the men came upon him.

She turned back toward them, no longer cautious of sound, and hoped that she and Reginald would be a match for the others. For a minute, it looked as if Reginald could handle all three by himself. Suddenly she heard a crack, and the crashing and splashing stopped as suddenly as it had started. She stopped too.

"You didn't kill him, did you?"

She recognized Webb's voice, and saw him turn a flashlight beam on Reginald's crumpled form.

"Gave him a headache. He's not bad hurt."

"Drag him up there."

Jane stood deathly still—much too close. Because the men had been so intent on the fight, they hadn't heard her noisy approach, and she arrived too late to help.

Her knees shook. She couldn't stop their shaking. When the men passed by, carrying Reginald toward the shed, she moved even closer, but with no idea of what to do. She watched helplessly as they entered the lamp lit area and dropped Reginald to the ground. He groaned and rolled his head but remained unconscious.

"Tie him up before he comes to," Webb shouted.

Lubin walked over to a tree and leaned a rifle against it. When he turned back to get a piece of rope, she saw the gun slide from the tree. It lay in the weeds, barely outside the circle of light, and she knew she must somehow get to it.

Lubin and Tomás tied Reginald's wrists and upper body. Relief flooded her for an instant. If they were tying him, maybe they didn't plan to kill him, but what *would* they do? In her pocket, she found her knife and worked one blade open. It would be ready if an opportunity came to cut his ropes. His help was essential. She couldn't subdue three men by herself, though she knew she would try if the situation grew any more desperate.

She inched in the direction of the rifle as Lubin and Tomás finished their job on Reginald and started to rise. A warning died on her lips as Webb's gun discharged two times. Lubin and Tomás dropped lifeless to the ground before her eyes.

When he aimed the revolver lower, she felt certain he intended the same for Reginald. With the rifle still too far away, she threw the rake at him and leaped in his direction. The rake did no harm, but it confused him for an instant, confused him until she reached him. Though no match for the strength of his long, powerful arms, her fury helped her hold her own. Using boots, elbows, and knees in a nontactical but energetic attack, she had almost gotten the upper hand when someone grabbed her from behind, wrenching her arms in the fierceness of the attack.

Pinned again, she let him carry her weight and lashed out with both boots at Webb. He backed out of reach, then dove in and grabbed her legs before she could do more damage.

"She's the girl, isn't she?" the man behind her asked. "Ha! They both came to us and saved us a bunch of trouble. Let's finish it tonight. Get the Mexican's gun and get rid of both of them. It will look like another drug shootout and everyone will die."

Webb released her legs and went for the rifle, but he couldn't find it.

"Where'd he leave it?" He turned the flashlight beam all over the area in his search.

Jane stopped her struggles and waited for the right opportunity to renew her effort. She couldn't see the tree where Lubin had left the gun. It was too far to the side of her range of vision.

"Forget it," the man holding her said. "I've got a better idea."

The pressure he exerted on her arms grew so unbearable she became light-headed. She tried to keep from passing out but started to fade in spite of her efforts.

"We meant to pick you up tonight, both you and Faircloth." The man's harsh voice in her ear brought her back. "Now we won't have to bother. It was supposed to look like the growers killed the nitwit snake lady who wandered onto their marijuana patch, and Faircloth killed his growers so he wouldn't have to pay them. Or maybe he was afraid they'd give him away. Anyway, he was going to get shot in the process and die out here too."

The man talked of their demise as if discussing the weather. She became horrifyingly conscious.

"We don't need their gun," he continued. "A snake will end Faircloth's life, right here and now."

Webb looked startled at the new plan, then beamed.

"That would work, Rich."

"Only if you can find a venomous snake. They don't hang from the trees, you know," Jane broke in, aware now that Richard Taggart held her arms.

"How about a rattlesnake? A big rattlesnake will kill a grown man like him, won't it?" Webb asked.

"It can, if it's large enough to inject a lot of venom and the wound goes untreated. But large rattlers aren't that common."

She wanted them to talk, anything to stall them. Surely Harris would guess where she went and would arrive there soon. Then a ghastly thought came to her. The big diamondback she caught the day she spied behind the shed had been missing, bag and all, when she came back with Reginald. She thought that they either killed it or threw it in the river. Webb answered the unspoken question in her eyes.

"We have all your bags. We planned to leave them beside you where you fell after the growers shot you. That would show everyone why you were back here and what happened."

Webb picked up her rake and raked the bags out of the shed, obviously scared to handle any of them. The Diamondback proved its aliveness and sent out a warning rattle.

Jane saw that Reginald, now conscious, had rolled onto his side. He watched them. His eyes met hers for an instant. She expected to see fear in them, knowing how he felt about snakes, but no fright registered there. He only looked at her sympathetically. She knew then that if he felt any fear, it was for her, not himself. Immediately his gaze shifted around their immediate area, and she knew he searched for some idea, some last resort, just as she did. At least they hadn't bound his legs—nor hers.

Webb trembled with fear as he pushed the bag close to Reginald's legs. He appeared fascinated as the snake rattled its warning repeatedly. The bag shook ominously.

Jane wished her captor, this man who bossed the show, would drag her closer. If she could get within reach of the bag, she could stomp it and kill the snake before it bit Reginald. But the other man, as fearful as Webb, backed up a couple of steps in fear.

Webb, evidently concerned that Reginald might use *his* boots on the snake, got a piece of rope to tie Reginald's legs. When Reginald saw his intentions, he kicked out, trying to knock Webb off his feet and trying to rise to his own at the same time. Webb recovered his balance and knocked Reginald back to the ground, tying his legs.

Now Jane felt utterly helpless. When they both had their legs free, she could still envision a tiny possibility of escape. But now . . . She looked at Reginald but saw no despair on his face yet.

Webb timidly pushed the bag against Reginald's leg, but Reginald moved quickly. If the snake struck, it missed. Webb made three more attempts, but Reginald warded them off by swift movements.

"Don't they strike through bags?" Webb asked, but Jane didn't answer.

She didn't want to rush the inevitable. Only *she* knew how enormously luck had played it part in the situation so far. Reginald probably didn't realize it himself, but *she* knew. The snake, now thoroughly excited, probably wouldn't miss again no matter how quick Reginald moved. She prayed for Harris to arrive.

"Open the bag and let it out," the man holding her commanded Webb. "You've got a rake. You can keep it from getting away. Sling it on top of him."

Webb visibly shook as he kneeled near the bag. "Bring her over here. Make *her* open it. I'm not gonna get bit."

The handle of Webb's gun protruded from his pocket where he had put it after shooting Lubin and Tomás. She wondered if the other man had one. If he did, it would have to be in his pocket since she could account for both his hands. Suddenly, Webb grabbed his gun and pressed it against her head.

"Open the bag," he ordered. "Let her go, Rich, I got her."

"If you plan to kill me anyway, why should I help?"

"Because you might get to outlive your friend here. You're

our only expert on snakes. You advise us."

"Open the bag, Jane," Reginald said.

She felt the hard steel against her temple and knew it wasn't a good time to fight. Maybe when the snake came out of the bag, and their eyes riveted on it—maybe then she could attempt something. When Rich released her, she turned to have her look at him and saw the face from the picture and from the factory that night. He was certainly Richard Taggart of Tagland Mills. She picked up the bag by the top and slowly untied the knot.

When she hesitated, Webb hollered, "Now drop it. Grab her Rich." He kept the gun against her head until Rich gripped her again. Putting away his gun, he picked up the rake and pushed it at the snake, which had slid out of the bag, intent on escaping.

The snake instantly coiled its body around toward him and struck out at the rake. Webb jumped backward. She could feel Rich jump too. She struggled wildly in another attempt to break free. Suddenly Webb scooped the snake up on the rake and tossed it at Reginald.

Reginald moved fast and managed to roll his body enough that the snake landed beside him and just missed him as it struck. Webb reached out the rake again and dropped the snake on top of Reginald before he could move away a second time. He rolled quickly, doubling his legs, but she saw the fangs connect with his leg right above his boots. He moved again and saved himself from a second bite.

Chapter 14

Water can cover a multitude of sins.

While the men watched fascinated, Jane again let Rich carry her weight as she lifted both feet and kicked Webb in the direction of the snake. He stumbled and let out a high-pitched scream as he leaped to the side. The frightened snake headed directly toward Jane in its haste to escape. Rich dragged her with him in an effort to get out of its path and Jane, struggling furiously, managed to free one arm.

She grabbed his hair with her free hand and kicked his legs with the heels of her boots in a frantic effort to break free. She had almost prevailed when Webb recovered from his fright and pointed his gun at her.

"Don't! You'll hit *me*!" Rich shrieked.

A piercing shot rang out from the direction of the river. Both men froze in position. Their faces registered their bewilderment, but Jane fought desperately on, not willing to lose the advantage she had gained. When a second shot sounded, she managed to break free. The two men bolted toward the swamp while Jane dove to Reginald's side and cut the ropes on his legs. He was on his feet before she could get to the ropes on his wrists and upper body.

"To the river, Jane. Run for the river."

Reginald ran with arms and wrists still bound, and almost collided with José, who stood there in mute anguish with Lubin's rifle in his hands.

"José, come quick!" Reginald commanded and rushed on toward the boats. José looked stunned, shaken, and Jane grabbed his arm and pulled him to the boats where Reginald already waited.

"José, take that boat. I'll get this one," Reginald shouted as Jane cut the rest of his ropes. "Get in Jane. I'll push off." He and José pushed their boats out into the current and started the motors almost simultaneously.

"I can handle it now. Please sit and don't move unnecessarily," Jane pleaded.

Reginald ignored her and called out to José, "Follow us—fast." He motored swiftly out into the river with José close behind.

Jane and Reginald's boat had a more powerful motor, but José managed to stay with them. Jane found an ice chest with a small amount of ice left and filled it halfway with water from the river.

"If you don't take off your boot, sit back, and put your foot in there, I'll go back for my snakes."

He slowed the motor, and José pulled beside them.

"José, let that boat go and climb in here. Run this one."

"Good boat. We keep. You want I tie . . ."

"One Jane is enough for me to handle right now. Let the boat go, José. I'll buy you another one if you want it. I'm trying to keep you out of trouble."

Jane helped him off with his boot. He wore lace-ups, no doubt remembering their day of mud filled boots. His leg already showed swelling. She immersed his foot and lower leg in the cold water while he got out his cell phone and called Harris, giving him brief directions. Just as Reginald put his phone back in his pocket, José handed him a large hunting knife from the sheath on his belt.

"You cut bite. Suck poison."

"*No*! Just leave me to my cold water. I have enough wounds for one night," Reginald gasped. He looked at Jane worriedly. "Do I need to do that . . . that *cutting* thing?"

She smiled encouragingly. "Most doctors don't recommend that anymore. Sit still and keep your foot lower than your heart."

"I don't know about you, Jane, but I was already built that way."

"Be still and rest."

He leaned back stiffly, and she felt his pain. Such a large diamondback would have injected a quantity of poison. Worse yet, he had exerted himself violently directly after being bit. That put the poison into his system quickly. Still, such a bite wouldn't necessarily kill its victim, especially if the victim received antivenom. She hadn't told their captors that Reginald wouldn't die instantly from such a bite. If they had known that, they might have beaten him to death or shot him with any gun available.

"José, pull into the first lit up place you see so we can confirm our exact location and call an ambulance. Whatever happens, you stay with me and don't say anything," Jane warned.

"Jane, when you and Harris go back for the cars, take José to my house and have him stay there. Harris has keys to my house."

They looked back at José and saw that the happenings had taken their toll.

"José. José!" Only after Reginald had called his name the second time did José look up. "José, we'll take care of Tomás. I'm sorry."

José nodded, and Jane saw the tears run down his cheeks. He pointed to a bridge ahead. Jane turned her flashlight on the area and saw a lone fisherman at the water's edge who told them their exact location. Jane made the calls, first to the ambulance and then to Harris who was almost there and had brought a patrol car with him.

The officer reached them in record time with Harris in his wake. He went immediately to Reginald.

"I've already called for plenty of backup. Now I'm at your service. I can use my siren to get you to that ambulance quicker. Let me help you into my car."

"I'll wait here for the ambulance," Reginald insisted though he looked gray and sick. "You follow Harris. Let him show you where they were. We don't want them to get away. You've got more patrol cars on the way, and they'll need your help and guidance."

"It's useless to argue with this man," Harris told the officer. "Let's get over there."

When the ambulance arrived, Jane and José rode in it to the hospital with Reginald. They were both still at the hospital when Harris showed up later that night.

"How is he?" Harris asked as they stood at the foot of his bed.

"Not good. He's sort of out of it. He keeps . . . g-going away," she said. "He should recover, but there's always risk. "I th-thought . . .is there someone we should notify? A relative, someone close—in case . . . just in case?"

She thought of the woman at his house. Though she hated to share Reginald with anyone right then, she understood that she had no claim on him and someone else no doubt did.

"I don't know who. I don't know if he has any family over here. He's never mentioned them if he has," Harris said.

She didn't want to say it, but she gulped it out anyway. "Girlfriend . . . fiancée . . . anything like that?"

"Not that *I* know of."

Exasperated with him and herself, she explained, "A woman at his house . . . about his age. She called him Reggie. I got the impression she belonged to him, or vice versa."

"I don't know who that could be. When was that?"

Harris's befuddled response exasperated her.

"The night we went after toads."

"She means Mirta, Victor's wife," Reginald announced with annoyed, sleepy voice and half-open eyes. "She stayed at my place for a while . . . after their house burned. . . . Later she decided it was dangerous around someone like me. Went to stay with relatives. . . . All women feel that way about me, even my housekeeper."

He closed his eyes and lapsed into unconsciousness, or sleep, she wasn't sure which.

"He's feeling sorry for himself. I think that's a good sign. What can I do to help now?" Harris asked.

"I'm worried about José. I don't want him to do anything rash. He's grief stricken over his brother. . . . R-Reginald means to look out for him," she gulped, still fearful he wouldn't be around to look out for anyone. "He's in the waiting room."

"I'll buy him dinner and give him some advice."

"Reginald told me to take José to his house, but I don't know if I should leave José alone yet."

"Right now I have to get your truck and Reg's car. I have Reg's keys, give me yours, and I'll take José with me."

"Thank you, Harris." She settled back on a chair and prepared to wait the night through.

"I said 'all women feel that way about me,' confound it," Reginald's voice rang out clearly in the empty room a few minutes after Harris left.

She rose and came to his bedside. "What?"

"You heard what I said. Now don't lie about it."

"All women feel *what* way about you?"

"That I'm dangerous to be around. Didn't you listen? Didn't you hear anything I said a minute ago? I'm sick, confound it. Try to pay attention. You could be hearing my last words."

"I bet a lot of women have wished that."

"Wh-what?"

"You know—wished they were hearing your last words."

"Blast it, Jane."

She grinned. He *must* be better. "Have you never married?" she ventured timidly.

"Was supposed to. . . . She was unfaithful to me. Thought I wasn't a dependable prospect for a long-term arrangement. She wouldn't wait for me."

"While you were out of the country doing your investigative work?"

He nodded his best irreproachable nod, his mouth tight shut.

"When you were hurt, and in trouble, and couldn't get home to her?" she asked sympathetically.

"Exactly." His self-righteous mien bordered on ludicrous. "I needed time to find myself, prove I was more than a rich man's kid. I couldn't help the blooming circumstances."

"She shouldn't have deserted you. People need time to find themselves, and you were a prisoner part of the time. She should have waited longer."

Jane didn't know if the woman should have waited or not, but she wanted to humor Reginald in his present weakened state.

"Fifteen Years?" He looked up at her with eyes full of self-pity and waited for her approval.

"You weren't in Zaire fifteen years . . . *were* you?"

"It wasn't just Zaire. There . . . there was that Yucatan incident before that. And the Irish pub investigations—that's where I g-got . . . I-I made a wrong turn. . . . I'd rather not show you *that* scar, and then . . ."

"Oh no, Reginald, no wonder she left you. Wouldn't one good adventure prove you were more than a rich man's kid?"

"I was rather rich. It took a lot of proving." He rolled over on his side and looked at her. "She didn't leave because of how long I was gone. She left because she found out about me."

"About this—this *danger* thing, you mean?"

"Correct."

"I never thought of you as particularly dangerous," Jane said somewhat dubiously.

He ignored her comment and rolled to his back. "She left because *I* suggested that would be the wise thing to do."

"I see. Just like that. Do women always do as you suggest?"

"The obedient ones do, and she was a perfectly accommodating woman. When I told her she shouldn't marry someone like me, she obeyed. . . . I'm sleepy, Jane. Quit talking so much."

He closed his eyes, and she felt sure he had dozed off again. She went back to her chair with a much lighter feeling. Although still a little out of his head, he was definitely recuperating. She tried not to look at the swollen leg, which seemed puffier every time she glanced at it. After a few more minutes, she called Harris, talking quietly so as not to disturb Reginald.

"Have they caught them yet?"

"I haven't heard. There must be ten or more patrol cars lined up along the highway here. The sheriff's department brought in the two boats and seized their cars. I imagine they'll be caught soon, if they aren't already."

"They're not woodsmen, and they're scared of snakes—I can tell you that much. But if they're desperate and can swim, they might try to cross the river."

"The sheriff's department prepared for such a possibility. I hear dogs too. But if these guys get out of the woods, it may be hard to find them. No one knows who they are yet."

"Harris, I told you who they are in the note I left you!"

"What note?" When?"

"I leaned it against your phone before I left your office. I couldn't reach you on your cell phone. You told me you had to come back to the office."

"I came back, but when I saw your truck was gone I didn't bother to go in. Who are they?"

"One of them is Richard Taggart of Tagland Mills. The other man, Webb, works with or for him. I don't know his real name or his position. Taggart is the one in the picture getting into Teeman's car. Taggart probably killed Teeman. Webb probably killed Victor. And Webb killed Lubin and Tomás."

"Jane, I'll call you back. I need to give out this information right away."

Jane could hardly believe no one had seen her note. She had waited futilely for help to arrive. Thank goodness for José and the shots that saved their lives.

A doctor came into the room to check Reginald, and Jane moved out into the hall. A few minutes later he assured her that Reginald was doing fine. She settled back on the chair again and dozed intermittently. It was much later when Harris and José came in. She walked out into the hall with them, but Reginald called them all back.

"Did they nab the Tagland boys yet?" Reginald asked drowsily, and Jane realized he had listened to her earlier phone conversation with Harris. Reginald never missed anything.

"*Just* got them. The chase ended up quite a ways downriver. They looked a sorry, miserable duo by the time the officers caught them."

"Jane, you could have left Harris a message on his phone, you know."

"I-I did."

"I don't mean leaning against his office phone. I mean on his cell phone."

"Yes—yes. I wasn't thinking straight. I guess I panicked. But he said he would come back."

Reginald looked at José, who hung behind Harris.

"José, come out where I can see you. José, why did you only shoot twice? Why didn't you keep on? I've wondered about it all night."

"Only two bullets for Lubin's gun. Maybe more Lubin's

pocket. I no get time look."

Harris grinned, and Reginald looked flabbergasted.

"Where were you while all this went on?"

"Tomás say wait other patch. Say I too young. But I come through woods. Watch like you say. Maybe get eighty dollars for watch Mr. Webb for you."

"Thank you, José. I'll pay you later. . . . I'm very . . . *very* sorry about Tomás. I want you to stay with Jane or Harris until I get home. Do you have a family? Do they have a phone?"

"*Sí*—I call later. I wait. . . . Maybe no call."

Jane understood how difficult that would be for him—to tell them about Tomás's death and maybe tell about the marijuana. Reginald must have read his mind too, because he motioned José to come close.

"Did you or Tomás ever plant Marijuana before?"

"No. But Lubin do much. He teach."

"Jane, Harris will give you my house keys. Take José there and both of you get some sleep. I promise to call you immediately if I start to die, but I plan to sleep now too." He fell asleep instantly.

When she and José got in her truck, she noticed that José looked extremely droopy again—his face thoughtful and sad.

"You just need some sleep José. You'll feel better then."

"No. No want sleep. . . . You think men take Tomás away? Maybe leave on ground."

"I'm sure they've taken care of him, José, but we can check if you like. If there aren't any patrol cars there, we'll go back in and have a look, but we mustn't risk getting caught. We'll have to drive on by if anyone's there."

Jane made sure she had a couple of lights with her before she and José drove back to Reginald's property. The place looked deserted, not a car or person in sight. She wondered if the officers had even seen the marijuana seedlings. They were small, and planted a good distance from the shed. All the fields had dense growth or swamp around them. Quite possibly, they had been missed.

She and José followed the branch to the river, and followed the river on to the scene of the murders. They found no sign of Lubin, Tomás, or anything—not even an empty snake bag.

José hung his head. "I like throw plants in river."

"We might get caught, José. We might get in trouble." She hesitated. Finally, touched by the gloomy look in his eyes, she said, "But I'll help if you want to try. We'll have to *run* down the rows if we want to get all of these seedlings out of the ground before daylight. The deputies could come back anytime. You might get caught and get in trouble."

"I no care. We work fast. Maybe all gone when police come back."

"All right, take my truck keys. Run back to my truck. I have big bags in the back. Bring them quick but watch for cars. Hurry. I'll start work here."

Jane ran down the rows, pulling seedlings from the ground as she went. They came out easily because the roots hadn't had time to set well, and she had a large pile by the time José got back with the bags. With both of them working, the job went quickly. They would fill a bag, dump it onto the bank at the water's edge, and throw the mound of marijuana as far out into the river as they could. The river was muddy from recent rains and the water always ran swiftly. The plants disappeared from sight almost instantly.

They removed all the plants from that tract and hurried on to the other one. They were both dirty and sweating profusely, but she could see that the work benefited José. His cheerfulness increased as each batch vanished into the dark water, and when the last plant disappeared, he actually smiled. Jane could hardly believe they had accomplished the task so quickly.

"Hurry, José. Let's leave quick. It's almost light."

They ran to the truck and started toward town as daylight broke. Five miles down the highway, they passed two patrol cars going the other way, and José ducked his head to the floor.

"José, you can come up. They're gone. The police might have taken pictures of the fields last night, but I doubt it. I doubt they saw them. If they didn't, then the evidence is all gone. We could get in trouble for doing this, but I don't think anyone will find out. No one saw us."

"Good. Much good."

When they got back to Reginald's house, Jane had only

half inserted the key into the lock when the door came open, and Reginald stood there waiting.

"Reginald, why aren't you in the hospital?"

"A hospital can't legally keep a healthy man who doesn't want to stay."

"You mean you broke out?"

"Only after I called here and got no answer."

"José and I couldn't sleep. We had some loose ends to tie up."

"In a pigpen?" He face registered his disgust.

"Something like that. I'm sorry if we caused you concern. You shouldn't be here."

"Why? It's my house."

"You should be at the hospital."

"You're both filthy. Where have you been?"

"José was concerned about Tomás. He wanted to make sure Tomás's remains weren't still down there."

"Did anyone see you?"

"No."

"Did you get them all?"

She looked at him shocked. "Y-yes."

"In the river?"

She nodded, not able to believe he knew what they had been doing. Then he laughed so violently, she began to worry about him and helped him to a seat on the sofa.

"You should lie down."

"I need to make some phone calls."

He stretched out on the sofa and propped his swollen leg on a pillow. First, he called Harris and arranged for him to come by his house at eleven. His next call was to his attorney, whom he asked to do the same.

"Now clean up, both of you criminals, and neither of you say a word about anything. You'll have time to get a nap before they get here. Take any bedroom you like. The housekeeper won't come back until the danger is past."

She heard him laugh again as they both left the room. In a minute his voice rang out, "Jane, come back here. I've meant to ask you something. . . . Didn't you tell me you went downstate to talk at some schools? Did you lie to me?"

"Of course not. I had two schools scheduled, but I had some extra time." She started to leave, and he called her back again.

"Tell me about Tagland Mills, Jane."

"I went there the first night. Happened to meet Mr. Taggart, only I didn't know who he was. When I looked at the enlarged picture last night, I recognized him. I couldn't reach you or Harris, so I decided to check your land to see if you'd stepped into some kind of trouble. When I found your car there, I sneaked back in to make sure you hadn't been captured or killed. I was much quieter than you were."

"I climbed up on a log for a better view. I didn't know it was rotten," he said indignantly.

"Fallen trees *do* rot. It's a swamp, you know."

"Are you all right, Jane? I shudder to think of what you've been through since you've known me."

"I'm fine, but I don't know how José is. You should think of something for him to do. It will help. He acted almost happy when we pulled up that . . ."

"You didn't pull anything up, Jane," he interrupted.

"You told me not to lie."

"I don't want you to lie. I don't want you to talk at all. Go clean up. I've never seen anyone who could get so dirty."

She started to leave, but he called her back again. "Jane, Mirta has a rather possessive manner about her. Was she the reason why you never came into my house?"

"I was told not to talk."

She left the room for the third time and smiled at his fury.

"Jane. Come back here. I can't get up and run after you. I'm sick, and you'll make me worse. Jane? Jane, come here, confound it!"

Jane showered and fell asleep almost instantly. José tapped on her door at eleven o'clock to tell her some men had come and Reginald wanted her. José had a new look of importance on his face that made her want to laugh. He handed her the suitcase that she kept in her truck and quickly rushed away as if he had to get back to duties of more consequence.

She searched for something suitable to wear and found the

white, knit dress she wore bowling with Cody. It at least looked clean, and its material didn't wrinkle.

The attorney advised them how they should handle the situation. At that point, it looked doubtful that anything would come up about the marijuana. Jane felt slightly miffed that they had left her out of their plans, but she knew Reginald did that to protect her.

"Have they found out for sure yet whether Taggart killed Teeman?" Harris asked.

"Absolutely," Reginald said. "Taggart said that Teeman caught him hauling off a load of drums containing toxic waste. He had no permit, and I guess he planned to dump them wherever. Teeman knew that Tagland Mills had former violations and that another bad report could ruin Taggart. Hence, he blackmailed him. Taggart said Teeman was a weasel—had eyes that saw everywhere and was bleeding him dry. Teeman had just stopped at Tagland mills and collected a payoff. Afterward, Taggart and Webb followed him to M P Pulp and Paper. When he came back to his car after an inspection there, Taggart shot him. The rest played out as we figured. Taggart saw Victor with his camera aimed in his direction, so he told Webb to follow him and take care of him."

"Would you get the phone, Jane?" Reginald asked as the ringing of his house phone broke into their conversation.

"Reduced to a secretary," she thought as she went to answer the call.

She returned in a few minutes carrying the phone. "Anna just got a call from a dentist who replaced a cap for a man fitting Webb's description. He replaced it Wednesday morning. He also said the picture you faxed of the broken piece matched absolutely."

"It's Friday morning. What did he think we were going to do? We warned him the man was dangerous and would probably give a fictitious name. Where on earth is this belated dentist located?"

"Here. Right in town."

"Here? *Here*? He could have saved us all of this! Why didn't he call?"

"He told Anna he meant to but it slipped his mind."

"Bring me that phone.... What's his name, Anna?... Anna! ... Give me his name! ... Anna! ... She hung up. My secretary hung up."

"She knows you well," Jane said, and they all had a laugh at Reginald's expense.

"Say, where is José? Did he go back to his home?" Harris asked. "He's a smart young fellow. I like him. Glad you kept him out of it. By the way, he hit me for a job. Told me he spies on people for eighty dollars a day. I don't know where he got an idea like that, but I'm tempted to take him up on it." Harris laughed.

"He's still here—relandscaping my property. That will keep him busy for a while and help him earn some money until we put this mess behind us. I told him what I wanted done in my yard. I'll let him use his own judgment. He probably knows better than I do what will look good. I had him take Jane's truck, and I gave him a considerable wad of cash. I want to see if he's trustworthy."

"With my truck?" Jane asked astounded.

"That truck would never tempt him. I referred to the *money*. I told him to work at his own pace, buy his own lunch, and sleep some more if he felt tired."

"Well, you'd better get some rest too," Harris suggested. "We'll leave you in peace. Make him rest now, Jane."

When Harris and the attorney left, Jane felt she should leave too. "I haven't been home in ages. I need to pick up the animals I left at Harris's office and take them home. I need to pick up some clothes too."

"That white looks nice. That's what you wore when you went out with Cody, isn't it?"

"I believe so. . . . You mean Cootie, don't you?" she asked innocently and saw the laughter in his eyes.

"Doesn't your hand feel a bit naked?"

"All of me feels good."

"Let's pop out for a minute and get a bit of dinner. I'm deuced starved."

"Are you up to that? I could fix you something here, and you could stay off of that leg."

"Blast it, Jane. I want to go out. I can bloody well prop my foot on a chair. You're so seldom presentable; I have to take advantage of it when I have an opportunity. You can drive though."

Dinner slightly overwhelmed her. She feared she would make

some etiquette error. It disconcerted her to sit across from him, and she wondered how to handle lobster and crab claws with a meticulous gentleman eyeing her every move. She couldn't just dig in with both hands. Soup would have been a better idea. She knew the proper way for soup and could have handled it admirably.

"Jane, I'd like you to do the last section of Victor's book. I've already okayed it with Mirta. I want you to devote it to waste disposal practices of farms, small businesses, and homes. Photos of those chemical cans we saw around the fields would be interesting. In a few days, when my leg's well, I'd like to go again with you."

"You want to see a snake again, after what's happened to you?"

"No. No snakes. I want you to take me back to where the beavers built the dam. I liked the beavers. Their lifestyle interests me. But right now I want to go to the airport and get my car back. Maybe someone who's not supposed to see us will walk past us again."

"Maybe we should check on José," she quickly suggested, changing the subject.

"Good idea. We'll stop by my house on our way," he said as they rose to leave the restaurant.

At Reginald's place, Jane immediately saw, with relief, that José had more than lived up to their expectations and trust. He stood proudly beside Jane's truck, which contained an abundance of shrubbery—proof he had been exceptionally ambitious. He also sported a broad smile and a brand new fedora that looked decidedly like Harris's, only black.

"I do much work. Spend much dollars . . . by Jove!"

It was apparent José learned quickly, and now he had *two* heroes to ape.

"V-very good, José." Reginald's face registered a strange expression, as if he suppressed immense amusement and strangled in the attempt. "I didn't mean for you to work right now. . . . I've been thinking, José." Reginald studied him seriously. "Would you like a vacation, a chance to visit your family in Immokalee? I'll pay for it."

José looked at him in disdain. "I like stay here. No family in Immokalee."

"Your driver's license says you live in Immokalee. Don't you have *any* family or friends there?"

"No . . . no live Immokalee. Brother, José, live Immokalee . . . long time. He no like Immokalee much. Take wife, bambino, and go back Mexico.

Reginald seemed confused. "Your brother . . . is . . . is named José too? I thought he was Tomás?"

"Cinco brothers. José is oldest. He no want I should go Floreeda. He say I too young, say I no like this place. I take José's license. Take José's letter. Come United States, come Floreeda. Now I José—United States citizen."

"Th-that's not exactly how it works Jo . . . Jos . . . what *is* your name? And how old *are* you?"

"In Mexico, I Alfredo. Here, I José. I have fifteen years soon, much soon."

"You're only fourteen years old?" He looked at Jane helplessly. "So now I'm harboring an illegal alien and a minor as well . . . and . . . and a marijuana farmer!"

"Come see work. I do much work. You like very much. Come see." He impatiently waved for them to follow him into the far reaches of the immense back yard. Reginald grumbled as he hobbled after them. Suddenly Reginald stopped dead.

"Jane, have I gone daft? Are those? Those aren't . . ."

Straight ahead of him lay a neat, green patch of marijuana seedlings. José stood self-importantly beside it, his fedora pushed back off his forehead.

"José, what have you done?"

"Do like you say. Plant *grass* here in bare place, you say. You give money, and I buy seedlings like Lubin . . . by Jove. Nice place here. Bloody high walls—no one see."

Reginald's eyes started to stream.

"José," Jane said, barely able to speak. "You th-threw all that marijuana in the river s-so you and Tomás could keep your good names."

"Throw in river so to help Mr. Faircloth. Police no find he grow marijuana. I like Mr. Faircloth. I save him from go jail—by Jove."

There is much virtue in men, little in herbs.
THE END

Jean James collecting reptiles with snake in bag

Wherefore Art Thou, Jane?

Jean James was active in many outdoor pursuits before becoming a full-time writer. She collected live mammals and reptiles for international distribution, collected live venomous snakes for antivenom production, and was involved in sundry wilderness construction projects. She also worked as a press agent, a songwriter, and was the captain of a small, leaky cabin cruiser. She is the mother of six children, the youngest, Mary James, being her co-author on this book.

jameswriters.com

Mary James (Mean Mary) at age 6

Wherefore Art Thou, Jane?

Mary James began life as a musical prodigy—could read music before she could read words and co-wrote original songs at age five. By age seven, she was proficient on the guitar, banjo, and violin, and entertained audiences across the US with her vocal and instrumental skills. Her life has been one long road show interspersed with TV, radio, and film work. She is also a prolific songwriter and the spirited host of Nashville TV show *Mean Mary's Never Ending Street.*

meanmary.com

Pate and Faircloth 2
The Inconstant Chameleon

Before JANE PATE and REGINALD FAIRCLOTH can plan a more permanent and more romantic future, they are besieged by guests from England. Reginald's father, Wilbur, and Reginald's old fiancée, Helen, at once take Reginald off Jane's hands and into Helen's arms.

Jane rides the back seat while these three moneyed individuals show her she must fight for her self-esteem. When she sets out to prove she can do more than catch snakes and write critter books, she discovers a far more vital matter awaiting proof. The plight of one missing homeless man turns into a shocking revelation of nursing homes full of victims and a doctor who will have wealth at any cost.

Her pride and her great exposé forgotten, Jane races to save the next victim. When Reginald finds Jane breaking into offices, cracking safes, and burying stolen money, he does the only thing one would expect from Reginald Faircloth. He plunges into the situation in his own reckless style and proves he has played this game before.

Look for the song
Wherefore Art Thou, Jane?
by *Mean Mary*
(*Year of the Sparrow* album)
available on iTunes, Amazon, and other select stores.

Jean James • Mary James